✫ Sideshow ✫

Sideshow

Ten Original Tales *of* Freaks, Illusionists, *and* Other Matters Odd *and* Magical

edited by

DEBORAH NOYES

CANDLEWICK PRESS

Introduction copyright © 2009 by Deborah Noyes

Compilation copyright © 2009 by Deborah Noyes

"The Bearded Girl" copyright © 2009 by Aimee Bender

"Those Psychics on TV" copyright © 2009 by Vivian Vande Velde

"The Year of the Rat" copyright © 2009 by Danica Novgorodoff

"The Mummy's Daughter" copyright © 2009 by Annette Curtis Klause

"When God Came to Kathleen's Garden" copyright © 2009 by David Almond

"The Shadow Troupe" copyright © 2009 by Shawn Cheng

"Cat Calls" copyright © 2009 by Cynthia Leitich Smith

"The Bread Box" copyright © 2009 by Cecil Castellucci

"Living Curiosities" copyright © 2009 by Margo Lanagan

"Jargo!" copyright © 2009 by Matt Phelan

First edition 2009

Library of Congress Cataloging-in-Publication Data

Sideshow : ten original tales of freaks, illusionists, and other matters odd and magical / edited by Deborah Noyes. — 1st ed.
    p. cm.
Contents: The bearded girl / Aimee Bender—Those psychics on TV / Vivian Vande Velde—The year of the rat / Danica Novgorodoff—The mummy's daughter / Annette Curtis Klause—When God came to Kathleen's garden / David Almond—The shadow troupe / Shawn Cheng—Cat calls / Cynthia Leitich Smith—The bread box / Cecil Castellucci—Living curiosities / Margo Lanagan—Jargo! / Matt Phelan.
ISBN 978-0-7636-3752-1
1. Short stories, American. 2. Curiosities and wonders—Juvenile fiction.
[1. Curiosities and wonders—Fiction. 2. Short stories.] I. Noyes, Deborah. II. Title.
PZ5.C103 2009
[Fic] —dc22   2008037420

2 4 6 8 10 9 7 5 3 1

Printed in the United States of America

This book was typeset in New Baskerville.

Candlewick Press
99 Dover Street
Somerville, Massachusetts 02144

visit us at www.candlewick.com

*For all who welcome the passing strange—
especially the authors, artists, editors, and designers
who've contributed to this series*

Contents

★ ★ ★ Introduction ★ ★ ★

In the 1800s and beyond, fairs, carnivals, and circuses fed the popular craving for the rare and strange. Traveling sideshows migrated from Europe to America and criss-crossed the United States for more than a century, flaunting savages and snake charmers, fire-eaters and five-legged sheep, illusionists and legless acrobats.

Unabashedly sensational, the sideshow aimed to shock and amaze, to rouse the voyeur in us—and freaks, short for "freaks of nature," filled that bill best.

Some freaks were congenital (dwarfs, giants, con-joined twins), and others were self-made novelty acts (contortionists and sword swallowers, glass eaters and human pincushions). But before professional medicine demoted many freaks from "marvels" to pathological specimens in the early twentieth century, few would have found the term *freak* offensive. In the 1940s, public opin-ion shifted from awe to embarrassment, but until then the sideshow was America's most popular form of enter-tainment, and to be a freak was to be a celebrity.

Today the concept seems cruel and exploitive. Activists speak of the "pornography of disability," and books and films like David Lynch's classic *The Elephant Man* have dramatized the agony and degradation many freaks suffered at the hands of a curious public.

But something of the old sideshow allure lingers for storytellers, and in these pages Aimee Bender cleverly updates the bearded lady. Annette Curtis Klause, Margo Lanagan, and Danica Novgorodoff offer sideshow mummies, dwarves, and monstrous zoological specimens. Shawn Cheng introduces an illusory shadow troupe, and Cecil Castellucci a bread box to rival the most bizarre of curiosity cabinets. Cynthia Leitich Smith lures us into an astonishing fairground subculture, and Vivian Vande Velde puts a high-tech spin on that old carny standard, the fortune-teller. A freak of another sort, the psychic sees what others can't, what perhaps should not be seen — just as God should not appear in an ordinary garden, as he does (or does he?) in David Almond's deceptively chilling entry. And in the grand finale, Matt Phelan sets himself the lofty goal of "freaking out the freaks."

We may quench our curiosity with the TV remote these days (or a quick Google search), but the world is still wondrous strange, and we're as curious as ever, as eager to make sense of it all, to (often erroneously) sort "normal" from not, "natural" from "unnatural," tangible from inexplicable. So step up for a healthy dose of weird delight, courtesy of ten master storytellers.

☆ Sideshow ☆

The Bearded Girl

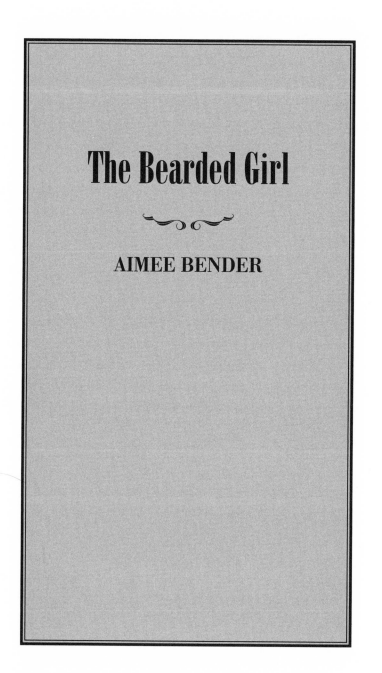

AIMEE BENDER

Mom bought me the razor when I was thirteen. It was not my birthday, but I came home from school at three thirty, after another truly crap day, the kind of day where you imagine space- and time-travel constantly. I kept seeing the spaceship, hovering on the grassy lawn, pointing a blue, beautiful laser walkway at me. "Molly," the aliens would say. "We have selected you. Come." And I even got a little pleasure out of the depth of the envy Baker Adams might feel, the envy and relief, seeing me walk across the lawn, past the flagpole, onto the sheer blue walkway, and up into the spaceship to project into the future, perhaps a future on a kinder and hairier planet.

I had walked the half hour home to avoid the whole bus rigmarole, and Mom had it for me as I walked in. It was wrapped in paper that was obviously from the pharmacy, being that it had CVS printed all over it in bright red letters.

"For you," Mom said, handing me the package. "I thought of you today when I was shopping. How was school?"

"Awful," I said. "The usual."

She flinched, but she pointed at the package, as a kind of emphasis, or answer. I sat down. I had the habit of stroking it — my face — a little, like Abe Lincoln. Like men do when they're trying to look introspective and smart. I had already developed that habit, even though at the time I was only thirteen and puberty had just hit, and my breasts were buds, and I had very little hair down there, but kind of a lot up top. It was soft on my chin, and curly. I see Ginny MacGinnis doing this with her ponytail constantly, petting it, but because it is her ponytail and therefore appropriate no one gives a hoot when all they do is point at me all day like no one in the history of the planet has ever had hair grow out of her face before.

I opened the wrapping, with some of the usual excitement about any kind of gift, and then just before I caught a glimpse of the packaging I knew what it was. I knew it because of Mom's look on her face, a look she was putting out into the air so fully that even without seeing it, I could see it. That look of worry and hope and eager desire to make me better, to change me, to make it all OK, to smooth. The curse of the parent, particularly for her, the single parent. Dad had left for Alaska when I was two, and I felt sometimes how I was supposed to be a good kid to prove to other people that she had done well on her own. And she had. I was a good kid, I just didn't want to prove it all the time.

I held up the razor in its fancy plastic packaging.

"So," I said.

"There's no reason why you can't use it," she said. "I know it's awkward, but I truly think it will make school easier for you."

She shrugged a little, perched on the edge of her chair, as if she'd practiced that line many times.

"Everyone has things to deal with, Mol," she said. "It's about *how* you deal with it."

I'd certainly heard that one before. Always a decent line, though a little less punchy in the retelling. But it was a nice kind of razor, an electric one, with circles made of metal and a plug-in setting adjuster, and it promised so close a shave it would turn me smooth as a stone. I didn't want to use it, because I had grown attached to the hair, which I'd now had for about two months. I just felt some kinship with it. But I loved my mother more, and her hope was too pretty and her effort too hopeful to be crushed so fast.

"Sure thing," I said.

★

The following day at school everyone laughed at me, clean-shaven, looking like a girl again, even with two braids down my sides, even with little pink bows on the tips of the braids, which I'd added for girly effect.

"What, did you shave or something?" asked Baker, and I said yes.

"With a razor?" he said, and I could see the flicker of jealousy cross his forehead, then, because he had only one hair, poking out of his cheek, and it would be years before more came to join it.

"No," I said. "With a rusty knife."

"You look weird," he said.

I looked normal, is how I looked, and in the school bathroom mirror it was strange to see me, the me of earlier, of two months ago when I'd had friends at lunchtime, and afterschool activities with friends, and invitations to sleepovers with friends. In class, they all started to adjust to me again, and they stopped calling me devilworm, which I really had hated, but because I am a redhead is an easy choice. I even started eating lunch with Deena again. She'd said she just couldn't stand looking at it, and it had made her want to throw up her lunch, but now she said it was fine. And although it pained me every morning to get up, shower, and shave, like the father I did not have, I was seeing the benefits pretty much immediately. Plus Mom's relief—the smile on her face!—was almost enough on its own.

On Tuesday I got a nice invitation with streamy

ribbons to Sally's birthday sleepover in a month, which would begin with a visit to the gymnastic studio, including some time on the parallel bars.

At night I could feel the tiny stubble growing in, even as I lay in bed, and I touched it. I didn't encourage it, but I wasn't mad it was there. Each morning I mowed it down, but the best part of my day was that part, just feeling, in bed, that I was still myself, that I was putting on a show during the day but that this was the real me, and somehow as long as *I* knew that, that it was a show, it was OK. I, like anyone in seventh grade, enjoyed the concept — and practice — of friends.

The hairs must've paid attention to that careful petting and patting at nighttime. And if hair has free will, then each follicle used its own, because the era of clean-shavenness did not last. I should've guessed it when I could feel the growing in third period, like I could literally feel hair pushing out of my chin. Each one a triumphant explorer, heading west, breaking through the force of the epidermal layer and plunging into air. By sixth period, a smattering of little curls. By home, the usual beard. Mom's face fell. "What happened?" she said, looking at me while my hand went up there to stroke the curls — and I did like how it felt, I did! Even though I also liked having that party invitation in my pocket. "It's speeding up," I said. "I can feel them, gaining speed." Mom rushed me to the bathroom, and I did a round with the razor again, and after she took me for my first manicure at Doti Lynn's, which was fun except I just felt funny, having someone dote on me like that, even someone whose named encouraged it. I vowed to Mom and myself to shave more frequently, and for about a week I shaved in the morning and at three p.m., which worked. But it was a slow, steady speeding up, and in a couple weeks I had to bring the razor to school and head to the bathroom twice a day, after third and sixth periods, and then at every single class break while other kids went to their lockers and talked and girls put on lipstick or lip gloss or brushed their bangs. I'd be in the back of the bathroom, with a hand mirror, frantically shaving.

Sally got her period. I got mine, too. I put in my first pad and shaved my chin clean.

"Are you a boy or a girl?" Sally said one day in the bathroom between classes. She was putting puffs of blush on her cheeks.

"Girl," I said. "Girl."

"I can't have boys at my party," she said.

"I'm not a boy," I said, and no one else was in the bathroom so I dropped my pants to show her the pad streaked with red. "Boys don't bleed there," I said.

She shrugged. Her freckles were so tiny, like someone had dotted them on her face with the pointed tip of a paintbrush. She obliterated a few of them with a circle of blush.

"Sorry," she said. "I asked my mom and she said no boys and nothing even close to a boy, and if you are not a boy, you are close to a boy. Or even a man," she said, "not even a boy. My mom said no men at *all*!" she said, and she ran out of the bathroom like I was going to do something to her, like I was a pedophile stalking the girl's bathroom instead of a girl her own age with her first wave of menstrual cramps that meant I was sent to the nurse's office and spent sixth period on her nurse's bed with its thin board of a pillow, resting.

I walked home alone. It was growing as I walked. I could feel those hairs pushing through chin skin again. I stroked them a bit as I walked, because it made me think a little more clearly. My brain seemed to ease up when I acted like Lincoln that way, which helps me understand why Lincoln kept the hair he did, and who's to say that he didn't make those fine choices for our country in part due to his facial participation? I walked and rubbed my chin and I thought, *I cannot keep shaving in between every single class. I simply cannot.* I rolled that thought around in my head for the whole walk home. By then it was growing so fast I would've had to hold the razor in my hand, near an electrical outlet or on a battery, the entire day. So I got home and went to the bathroom and put the razor in a drawer. Mom was at work at the diner, so I had a little moment with the razor where I thanked it for trying but told it that my beard had won.

Then I faced myself in the mirror and nodded. "You won," I told my face.

Is it so wrong to say there was a tiny glimmer of relief? Maybe bigger than tiny, even? It was, after all, my face, plus I kind of liked the beard, as I've said. Against my will, I liked it. If a gun was put to my head, and I was asked, "Tell the truth: do you like the beard? And if you lie we will kill you." I would have had to say that I liked it. I worried it would get really long, like an old-man beard, like the one on the man on the inside of a peanut, the Moses/Jesus man. But once I'd put the razor away, the beard slowed back down to its usual growth rate—which was the regular rate for men, I think—as if it had only announced its presence more aggressively when I was mowing it down with equal force. It returned to its usual state of chin, upper lip, and bottoms of cheeks, in brief red curls, hanging lightly but not too long. Trimming did not seem to be a problem. It was quite a neatly laid beard, the follicles spreading out in a nice map on my face; they did not climb up under the eyes or go way down the neck, but kept tidily to the jaw and lower cheek and upper lip. I gave up on the concept of friends. Sally's party came and went. Within about two months, after rounds of songs about devilworms led enthusiastically by Baker, I told my mother I could not stand school anymore, and I left to join the circus.

★

When I was two, Dad had left to go to Alaska, so it was a family tradition: hightail out of the small-town world and go someplace more wild. For Dad, this involved elk and moose, a trek that did not include people. *I have trouble with people,* he wrote me in a note I had and held until I turned ten, when it said, on the front, that I could read it. *Dear Molly,* it said. *Happy tenth birthday. I imagine you're a very nice kid,* he wrote. *I just have trouble with people and I get along much better with trees and elk so I'm going to go save some of those. Your mom is terrific—if I could pick a person, I'd pick her, and I did, but she's still a person. Even this letter will take me two weeks to recover from. I always seem more comfortable than I am. Just know your first word was* Dot, *which I thought was neat, and sounded something close to* Dad, *but maybe in German.*

Sincerely, your Dot

Well now that was a letter I read a million times. Each night before bed, and each morning when I woke up. He sounded so sweet in it. I showed it to Mom, who teared up a bit as she read it over. She shook her head. "He was so good to the squirrels outside," she said. "You wouldn't believe what it was like when dogs saw him. Their tails went nuts. Plunking on the sidewalk! I'd never seen anything like it."

She plucked another tissue from the box.

"He was a terrible, terrible husband," she said. "Not a good father. He didn't like to be in the same room as either of us. He often slept outside. He liked you when you couldn't talk, but as soon as you started to talk, he panicked. He would run out of the room. You would call after him, 'Dot! Dot!' He told you to *shhh* sometimes, when you were just a year old.

"Shhh," she said, imitating him. She shook her head again.

"Bummer," I said, because being a mute was never even a remote possibility in my future.

"Do you think he'll ever come back to visit?" I asked that day, on my tenth birthday, when I read the letter for the first time.

She leaned her head to the side, and her eyes were very kind on me.

"I doubt it," she said. She gave me a hug. She said she was sorry.

"It's OK," I said, even though we both knew it was something sad I'd carry around for a long time.

My own venture to the wild was not for moose and elk but for people who were natural and unusual in a distinct enough way to make some cash off of it. The tall, the knobby, the convex, the overly flexible. There was only one easy circus option, a traveling circus, but it didn't travel far. It ran a circuit of about seven towns, all in the same state, this state, and it was not particularly famous or fancy. No elephants, no lions, no acrobats. One gymnast, a very tall man who wore a clown nose and did morose juggling, and a bear cub who liked to sit on a stool and clean its fur. The ringmaster was a high-school dropout who had loved debate club, so his ringleading speeches were combative, like "Why are you here? Why come to the circus? Is it a freak show? Or is it our truest selves?" and then he'd go back and forth for ten minutes with rebuttals and so forth. Occasionally he snuck in political themes, and once the entire audience walked out before any show had even begun when he starting yelling at himself back and forth about euthanasia. Just didn't fit the mood. Luckily, we charged extremely low prices, as in cents. We had those coin machines that would turn coins into dollars, and people would get a ticket by pouring in piles of pennies. For this reason, we had decent audiences. Sometimes people would rather get rid of their piles of pennies than keep them spilling over in a dish, and they sat at the show as a kind of afterthought, with pockets light and airy.

I had to wear an evening dress, which was funny for me, since I wasn't even a lady yet; I was thirteen, the Bearded Girl, but they thought an evening dress with tons of rainbow sequins would work well in contrast, and I wore my hair in those braids, and then, of course, the pièce de résistance on my chin. I first wrote a speech about masculinity and femininity. It was all Jungian, animus, anima, and I was as proud of it as anything I'd ever done in school, but the ringmaster said it was too highfalutin. "Just talk about beard itch," he said.

"You're highfalutin," I said.

"I won the debate club's trophy four years in a row," he said, grimacing. "I've earned it."

I didn't feel much like debating about that, what I'd earned versus what he'd earned, or whatever *falutin* might mean anyway, so I sat on my stool in my rainbow sequins and talked about school and the teasing and the razor. At the end of my monologue, I shaved a portion of it off. "Come back tomorrow," I said, "and it will be back!"

They liked that trick. Seemed to prove something to people, that it grew, and the ringmaster liked it because it encouraged repeat visits.

"This is no beard wig," I declared to the throngs of thirty, sleeping and swaying in the small sets of bleachers.

Mom came every night. Just like she had when I was eight and had played Lucy in the Charlie Brown holiday play. I was a good Lucy, had a big mouth when I needed to, which is why my father would've never lasted in our household. Mom liked to see me on the stool and hear me tell stories about school, and since I'd clammed up a little with her about school, as most teenagers do, it was kind of her way to find out what was going on with her daughter. Then she'd wait as I changed and drive me home. She'd set up a tutor for me in the mornings, the one who'd given me Jung to read—Sheila, who was a budding feminist in college, a newly declared Women's Studies major who also brought me all her Simone de

Beauvoir papers. We read passages aloud together. Most of it I didn't get, but I told her I had a kind of firsthand knowledge of ambiguity that might make the work more accessible to me than to most thirteen-year-olds; she sipped her diet soda and agreed. Sheila came to the circus too sometimes, with whatever girlfriend or boyfriend she happened to be going out with at the time. She liked to show me off, in mostly a sweet way. Since I'd gotten so much flack from my peers, I didn't mind a little positive objectification.

I had been working there for about six months, making a decent paycheck—something to put in the bank for college, where I would take my own series of Women's Studies courses, maybe even writing a paper on the evolution of the beard, I thought—when Baker Adams came to the show. I spied him in the ticket line. I hadn't seen him since I'd left school—hadn't said bye to Deena or Sally or him or anyone, because not a single one of them had earned a sense of closure, as far as I was concerned. If they felt a little guilty for the rest of their lives, that seemed pretty fair to me. Sooner or later, everyone runs into a body that won't do exactly what you want it to.

But I never expected Baker to be the one to show up. In his ripped jeans and old sneakers. With his messy hair and scrunchy nose. I hadn't left any forwarding address, or made any big announcement, so it would've taken some legwork for him to figure out where I went, and I could tell he wasn't just there for the circus itself because he was waiting outside, smoking a cigarette during the morose clown's juggling, and he only entered the big top when I took my seat on my stool, in my sequins. I told my stories, which, of course, included him, though I never named anyone directly. I called him Butcher instead of Baker, for example. I talked about bullying. And feeling isolated from everyone. And feeling ashamed, at first. And how it had just showed up one day as part of my puberty.

"I like it," I said as I neared the end of my talk, scratching my chin. "Can't help what you like," I said.

A few people asked questions at the end, because we liked to incorporate a little Q and A into my portion, especially, the ringmaster said, since I had a very engaging way of opening up and people liked to hear my experience. "You're disarming," the ringmaster said, and that was the only compliment I ever got from him, or from anyone, really, since the beard, so I looked it up in the dictionary, wrote it on a paper, and taped it into my diary. During the Q and A, I often got questions that were a little too personal, about if I got my period, or if I had boy parts or girl parts down below, and I'd just point to the sign over my head, the one that said BEARDED GIRL, and say, "Do you think that means something different?" And usually I'd cross my legs.

This time, I saw Baker's hand go up, in the back row. Baker, leader of the pack. Who had called me the devil from the first day I arrived with even just peach fuzz on my cheeks. "Devilworm!" he'd said, since earthworms are asexual. "Devilworm!" the class echoed. Baker, whose dad was in jail, whose mom worked the night shift as security at an office building, and who'd spent every night in his house alone since he was seven. His hand was tentative but strong, like he knew he had to ask this question but he was scared to anyway. The only thing that gave me the wherewithal to call on him was the knowledge that this was my turf, and if he was his usual jerky self, I could sic the tallest, most morose clown on him as he left and he could get a little roughed up by the big red nose.

"Yes?"

"Hi," Baker said. His voice had just changed — it was mostly low, a little crackly. "I have an ethical question."

"OK." I crossed my arms. I didn't want to seem too into it.

"What if," he said, "what if you regret something about the way you treated someone. What can you do?"

"You're asking me if I did that?"

"No," he said. He shook his head vigorously. "What if I did that," he said. I stared at him. I felt, for a second, like we were in the last scene of a movie and the music was about to sweep us away as we fell in love. I did not want to hold to any script like that.

"What could I do?" he asked.

"You could apologize," I said.

"OK," he said.

"How'd you treat the person?"

"Bad," he said. "I've learned something big since then."

"What's that?"

The audience craned back their heads to look at him, to see if he had something girly going on, like a full set of breasts, paired with this newly male voice. But he looked just like regular Baker—brown hair, scruffy eyebrows, crooked teeth, all boy.

"It's private," he said.

I shrugged. "Well," I said. "For me, it wasn't private. I would've loved it, if it had been private, but it was very public. So why don't you just say?"

He wobbled a little in his seat.

"Can't," he whispered.

"Fine," I said, trying to sound annoyed. "You should apologize, though. A lot. And let other people know you're sorry. That's a start."

"OK," he said.

"You could give gifts, for a while," I said. "Nice gifts."

"OK."

The heads swiveled back to me. Baker's hung low. All he'd done was ignite and thwart curiosity. A little girl in the front row raised her hand and asked if I wanted to marry a girl or a boy when I grew up. I smiled at her sweetly and said marriage was an institution, and so far, institutions and I did not mesh so well.

★

After the show, I went to my mini-tent to change. Mom was waiting for me in the car as usual, reading a mystery series she loved about a cop in Alabama who liked to unearth old unsolved mysteries post–Civil War. "It's history and suspense at once!" she said, every time, in the middle of the series. She was like a perfect advertisement for the writer. She'd also forget the plots and reread them and be surprised all over again, which is a fine and frugal quality in a mystery novel fan.

Baker was waiting for me outside the tent, so once I'd hung up my dress and changed into my sweatshirt and jeans, I found him, smoking another cigarette, awkwardly shifting from foot to foot. We stood staring at each other.

"Hi," he said.

"So what's the secret?" I said.

He hung his head again, and it was really like he was a different kid, and I felt older than him, which was weird because I wasn't. But it was like I'd already gone through something he was just starting to go through, and against my will, like my interest in my own beard, I felt like I didn't loathe the new Baker so much.

"I'm really sorry," he said. He kept eye contact even though it was clearly hard for him. His eyes were squinty, but they didn't flinch. "I was awful to you."

"True," I said.

"I'd never seen a girl with a beard before," he said.

"Me neither."

"I will tell everyone at school that I saw you and you're nice."

"Aren't you kind," I said.

"Want to go to the middle-school dance with me?"

"No."

"OK," he said. "Just I'd be proud to go with you."

"What's happened to you?" I said, shaking my head and laughing.

"I am turning into a cheetah," he said.

I laughed, more.

"A cheater?" I said. "Weren't you already?"

"A cheetah," he said. "Ah. Ah."

"Like the cat?"

"Yeah," he said.

"You look the same," I said, peering at his face.

"At night," he said. "At night I'm a cheetah."

I laughed again. I couldn't help it. He still sounded like someone from Brooklyn.

"Like a werewolf?" I said, starting to walk to Mom's car.

"Kinda," he said. He fell into step beside me. "Except I'm really fast. I just run around town. If someone spots me, they'll shoot me. I can't help running. Last week I woke up and I was by the side of the road, in Lafferton."

"That's *far*," I said.

"I know." He shook his head. "I was asleep, by the side of the road. It was cold. I took the bus back."

We walked in silence for a few minutes.

"So what do I do?" he said.

"I have no idea," I said.

"I tried to tie myself to the bed," he said. "But I chewed through the rope."

"Have you eaten a person?" I said.

His face dropped, low, filled with horror. "Do cheetahs eat people?"

"I don't know," I said. "Don't they?"

"I'll get a metal chain," he said. "I'll chain myself to the bed."

"How do you know you're a cheetah in the first place?" I said as we approached my mom, who was tucked up in her hatchback reading.

"I glimpsed myself in the mirror," he said, "on the way out."

We paused at the car. Mom didn't see us yet. Behind us, we could hear the nightly dismantling of the sound system, which had to be stored in a lockbox overnight.

"So," I said, sighing. "You want to come over for dinner?"

With a fast motion, he used the side of his sleeve to brush at his face, like he was crying. Weird, how things change. Weird. I don't even know why I asked, it just seemed like the thing to do. He said he'd be honored. He thanked me. We watched Mom in the car bubble, turning pages rapidly. She was two from the end, so we waited patiently outside, and when she finished, she looked up, her face glowing.

"It was the pet store owner!" she said, delighted.

"I remember that one," I said, opening the car door. "He'd been hiding the bodies in the back of the store?"

"How did you know?" she said, kissing my cheek. "Nice job tonight, Mol. Who's this?"

"This is Baker Adams," I said. "He was mean to me at school, but now he's being a little better."

Mom eyed him with a mom's suspicion, part of her job.

"It's OK," I said.

"Is this the one you call Butcher?" Mom asked, her voice hardening.

I looked at Baker. His eyes still a little red. His story about being a cheetah, whatever that meant.

"No," I said. "That's someone else."

He hung his head. He seemed slayed by my kindness, which was flattering. I told him he had to ride in the hatchback part, the part that wasn't even really a seat. He said fine. We drove along. Mom changed radio stations a few times. The truth was, even without his new problem, and his new resolve, Baker had far less pull on me now; once you decide you don't mind the thing everyone hates you for, none of it matters in the same way.

When we got to my house, Mom went to the bedroom to put things away, and I commenced chopping carrots for the salad. I gave Baker a bowl and told him to rip up the lettuce and put it in there.

"I bet it's nice, sometimes, being a cheetah," I said.

"No," he said.

"Isn't it a little fun?"

"It's all bad," he said.

"I don't know if I really believe you," I said once I'd swept the carrots into the bowl and started opening the can of garbanzo beans, which always gave our cat the tantalizingly wrong message.

He shrugged. He ripped the lettuce too small. Had he never eaten a salad before? Each leaf bit was the size of a quarter.

"No," I said, looking at the bowl. "Here." I showed him the proper size. "Oh," he said, nodding OK. "Do you never eat salads?" I asked. "No," he said. I gave him a cut of carrot. "Do you recognize this?" "No," he said. He ate it. "Crunchy," he said, bobbing his head. "What do you eat?" I asked. "I eat a lot of frozen hamburgers," he said. "Yum."

We ate a few carrots together, then. Nothing made me forgive Baker more quickly than seeing him rip lettuce into pieces so small like that. No transformation into animals, no out of nowhere apologies, no invitations to the dance. I gave him a garbanzo bean and he drew back like it was an alien, or snot, or a tiny organ from the body, chucked up.

Mom was busy in her room, opening and closing drawers.

"Can I touch it?" he asked.

"The garbanzo bean?"

His hand hovered in the air, near my face.

"It," he said.

He was looking at me with big eyes, unsquinted, and for some reason I knew then that he wouldn't come over again. I didn't know if he'd made up the cheetah story or not—I was willing to believe it but who knew; all I knew is that it was kind of a one-time moment, this. Baker Adams, in my house, having an encounter with me and with carrots.

"Sure," I said.

I put down the can of beans. The cat leaped up on the cutting board to watch. Baker was standing on the other side of the kitchen counter, and very, very slowly, he stepped closer and placed both hands on my face. He was gentle with his palms and thumbs as he smoothed the hair down on my cheeks, over my upper lip, over my chin, and all I felt then was how my father had left to go to Alaska, and how Baker Adams's father was in jail for some dumb crime like cheating, everywhere, with everyone, with sex, and money, and more, and for a second we were there with our missing fathers, him touching my beard like that, smoothing down my cheek with his palm.

"It's softer than I thought," he said.

"It?"

The cat flopped over on her side. He kept one hand on my face and started scratching her belly with the other. She purred, loudly.

"You," he said.

After a few minutes, Mom came in from the other room and we all ate dinner together. Baker helped clean up, did a nice job wiping down the forks, and I saw him to the door. He had not brought his bike, so he had a long walk home. I told him I could ask my mom to give him a ride, but he said it was OK. "I have a lot to think about," he said. The cat tried to sneak outside but I scooped her up, cradling her in my arms, and he seemed grateful that I was nice to the cat, as if on some other day he might come up to the door as a cheetah and I'd scratch between his ears instead of shooting him.

"Good luck," I said.

"Thanks," he said. He bobbed his head up and down, like there was something he wanted very much to agree with.

I let the cat down as he walked away, down the sidewalk, into the dark night. She followed him for a while. I waited, looking at the moon, thinking, and then I whistled. She's a cat, but she's smart. She listens. After a few minutes she came scampering back and ran into the house. I followed her in and closed the door.

Those Psychics on TV

VIVIAN VANDE VELDE

From the first time I saw one of those psychics on TV—
telling things about people, chatting with their long-lost
relatives—I was hooked.

"Cody," my mother used to say to me, "you know
all that communing-with-the-spirits-beyond stuff is just
hogwash."

"Most probably so," I'd answer. "But it's still interesting."

"Just so you know," Mama would say.

"Yes'm," I'd say back.

We couldn't get the TV picture so good. Sometimes
you couldn't hardly be sure if there was one TV psychic
or four. To get good TV reception at the trailer park,

you really need cable, and Mama's paycheck was already stretched awful thin, barely enough to cover the rent and the groceries. And Daddy's support checks didn't come in what you might call regular.

But the sound on the TV worked fine, and those psychics, they talked a good game.

There was this one guy, a Texas guy like us, who had his own TV series. He'd say something like, "Someone in the audience has someone done passed, and that someone goes by the initial of W. This here person was a military man, or he was in law enforcement—one or the other—but there's a uniform of that sort."

If nobody spoke up right away, that psychic would keep right on talking: "Maybe this man wasn't actually in the armed forces or police, but just had a real interest, and that's what the uniform signifies." And if still nobody reacted, he might say, "Now, maybe the official name on this man's birth certificate don't start with W. Maybe that's a nickname, or a pet name, something you or other people called him by. Come on, now, don't be shy. Who knows W?"

Then, sure enough, someone in the audience would rise up and announce, "That's my uncle Lloyd. When I was a baby, I wasn't so good at pronouncing the letter L, so I always called him 'Woyd.' But that part you said about being interested in the military? My uncle was writing a book about the Civil War."

And the audience would murmur in appreciation

at how deep the psychic's knowledge went, even though my thirteen-year-old self kind of felt that the psychic had been fishing.

"Yes," the psychic would say to Woyd's nephew, "Your uncle misses you and says not to feel bad, because he knows you didn't mean it. I'm getting a feeling here like . . . did you do or say something harsh, either when you were a child or more recently? Is there something you might have regrets about?"

And Mama next to me on the couch would snort, "Like there's anybody who doesn't have regrets."

Mama was of the opinion that half the people in the psychic's audience were down-on-their-luck actors who'd been given specific stories then planted there, and the other half were gullible fools.

"Not to mention," Mama would add just about every time, "there *is* such a thing as a program editor to cut out the really boneheaded things this guy says, where everybody goes, 'Nuh-uh, you're *so* wrong.'"

I told her, "That's why *we* should go and be in the studio audience. We could see if they make us fill out questionnaires before the show starts, and see if his people are feeding him information." Mama had told me that one TV psychic had gotten caught with an earpiece and an assistant who was wandering around the crowd while people were waiting in line, and this assistant was all the while whispering into that psychic's ear all the things everyone was saying.

I reminded Mama that there was a psychic coming to town in the fall—October 17 to be exact. This was a different one, a lady psychic who didn't have her own TV show. But she was going to be at the War Memorial Arena. That's what the posters all around town said. She would give two sessions with a whole audience, one at 2:00 p.m., and one at 8:00 p.m. But she would be available for the following three days for private psychic consultation—that's what the posters said, PSYCHIC CONSULTATION—for a nominal fee, which you could pay by cash, money order, or with your credit card.

"Oh, Cody," Mama said, "you know we can't afford tickets."

'Cause I had only mentioned the public sessions, never even brought up the psychic consultation, knowing if I did Mama would just say, "Cody, this interest of yours in psychics is beginning to border on the unhealthy." And she would of turned that TV right off.

So all I said was, "Well, sometimes the radio station gives away free tickets." And when Mama looked doubtful, I added, "And, just in case we don't win those, I *have* been saving up my allowance money."

Mama rolled her eyes but let it pass. "What, exactly, are you hoping for?" she asked me.

I got out the picture I'd chosen. It was of me, last summer, standing next to Jeffrey, my counselor from camp. I told Mama, "I would make up a story to tell everyone in the crowd while we're waiting to get in—just in case that psychic has spies. I'd show Jeffrey's picture and say, 'This here is my older brother, Max, who got killed when he was run over by a drunk driver in a pickup truck this past winter.' And if the psychic calls on us and says anything about good old Max, we'll know for sure she's a fraud, and then we wouldn't have to wonder anymore."

Mama looked a bit headachy at the talk of a dead, run-over son for herself. But all she said was, *"Anymore?"* Then she said, *"I'm* not wondering at all."

But now—what with one thing and the other—here it is fall, here it is October 18, and here we are, me and Mama, with ourselves visiting with that lady psychic after all. And we aren't at the War Memorial Arena, which was yesterday anyway; we're in the room she has at the Hill Country Hotel and Bar-B-Q—not the room she's *staying in,* of course, but the room the hotel has set aside for those private psychic consultations of hers.

It's a wonder no matter how you look at it.

Mama doesn't say anything. She's brought that picture of me and Jeffrey, the one that—ever since that day I told her my plan—we called "the psychic entrapment device." But she doesn't point Jeffrey out as my brother, Max, when she sets it down on the table.

The psychic, who looks a lot older than she does on her posters, ignores the picture. She acts like she doesn't even see me, but adults are like that: most often, a kid might just as well be invisible, unless he's misbehaving.

The first thing the psychic says is, "Now, you need to understand that communicating with those on the other side is not like you and me sitting here across from each other having a conversation, hearing each other's words and seeing each other's faces. Sometimes those who have passed use words, but their voices are faint, so most often they share images with me."

While me and Mama are nodding our heads to say we understand, she continues, "Remember, I'm not the one they're trying to reach—they're just going through me. Imagine someone who doesn't speak Spanish having to repeat a message in Spanish. So, when I'm explaining to you what's happening, I may well be misinterpreting. For you to get the full benefit of this reading, you may well have to help me out. If something doesn't seem to make sense to you, tell me, and maybe if I explain it a different way, or if we explore the possibilities together, you'll go, like, 'Aha!' I don't want you to lose faith just because of my limitations."

"All right," Mama says.

So much for the plan I'd worked out where we would say nothing and try not to react to what she would be saying.

I think it's unfair of the psychic to be so reasonable and personable and coming right out and admitting she isn't perfect. Not to mention so politely asking *us* to help *her.*

Now the psychic leans forward and taps the picture

of me and Jeffrey and says, "This is your son, isn't it? That you want to reach out to, on the other side?"

Mama ducks her head and doesn't answer. The psychic says, "Someone is coming to me. He says his name is . . . Bubba."

"My son's name isn't—" Mama corrects herself, "wasn't Bubba."

"I know," the psychic tells her. "But Bubba is stepping forward as the spiritual medium. He says he knew you and your son in life. Did you know a Bubba?"

I expect Mama to snap, "This is Texas. *Everyone* knows a Bubba."

But Mama behaves herself and admits, "Bubba was our neighbor at the old house, before my husband left us. Bubba and Lettie. You could tell he had high blood pressure by his coloring, and by his temper. He may well have died in the five years since we moved."

I want to poke Mama. I want to say, "Too much information! Make her work for it. Don't give stuff away, or we'll never know if she's for real."

I'm watching the psychic watch Mama. Mama said that Daddy left us, which could sound like it means he died, when all he did was run off with Velma, the night manager of the 7-Eleven.

But if the psychic is getting all her information from Mama rather than from Bubba-on-the-other-side, still she doesn't take a wrong guess and prove it.

The psychic says, "Bubba indicates he can tell from

your aura that you are a bit skeptical. And that's fine, honey. *I* was skeptical when the power first started revealing itself in me. All I'm asking is that you keep an open mind. Can you do that?"

Mama nods, because what else can she do?

The psychic says, "Bubba wants us to prove to you that this is him speaking. He's sending me mental pictures about when he and his wife—Lettie, right?—lived in the house next door to your family."

So far, I think, all she's doing is taking information Mama already gave her, and presenting it as though she's the one coming up with it. I notice Bubba isn't forthcoming with Mama's son's name.

The psychic says, "He says the house was white—"

Mama is shaking her head. "Our house? It was stone."

The psychic says, "Maybe he's showing me his and Lettie's house?"

"Light green," Mama tells her.

"I'm sure he's showing me white," the psychic says. "Maybe he's showing me your *next* house will be white, or maybe he means the inside of the house, that the walls were white."

Mama is suddenly nodding. "So safe, so boring. I was always telling Nolan we needed to get brighter colors, but he never got around to it before he run off."

Mama doesn't know how to play this game, I think. She's too nice, and—despite her doubts—she doesn't want to embarrass the psychic, doesn't want to be in her face about her being wrong.

"Yes," the psychic says, "that's what Bubba is showing me, the white-painted walls . . . inside your old house . . . where — remember — I've never been . . . that you wanted Nolan to paint, but he didn't. Bubba says there was color outside the house, though . . . a garden . . . bluebonnets by the road . . . a Bradford pear . . ."

No kidding. It helps that bluebonnets are the Texas state flower and grow wild everywhere. And Bradford pear trees are about as common as guys named Bubba.

But Mama is adding, "The wisteria bush . . ."

And a half moment later, the psychic is saying, "wisteria . . ." as though *she'd* just come up with it, and wasn't simply repeating.

So for the next few minutes, the psychic gives rapid-fire snippets of information, as told to her by Bubba. Some of it's kind of broad and general ("There's something he's trying to tell me about some sort of repair that was needed . . ."), some is downright wrong ("Porch? Sunroom? Never mind, maybe that's something in your future. . . ."). But some of these comments are right, and I can see Mama is latching onto those.

Then the psychic says, "I'm seeing something about your son and the number six. Does the number six mean anything to you? It could be a month, the sixth month, June . . . or it could be the sixth day of a month . . . or it could be a year ending in the number six. . . . Anything significant there?"

"Nolan's mother's name was June. . . ." Mama offers.

"No, that's not it," the psychic says, which is a surprise to me, that she would turn down a connection Mama is so valiantly trying to make for her. "This is to do with your son. . . . Not born on the sixth of a month?"

But even as Mama is shaking her head, the psychic continues, "No, Bubba's saying that's not it. Nothing in June? Something that happened in June, not necessarily this year . . . maybe a family trip or the anniversary of an important event . . . the start or end of something . . ."

"Well, in July every year," Mama starts, "we'd go—"

"Six," the psychic repeats. "When your son was six years old . . . sixth grade?"

Mama gasps. "Cody was in sixth grade when he fell and broke his arm, and we took him to the hospital—" She swallows hard and bites her lip.

Mama is upset at the memory of me in the hospital, and the psychic has a self-satisfied expression in her eyes, so I can't resist giving the woman a little kick in the shin under the table.

She looks startled, but only tucks her legs closer to her chair, probably assuming Mama, agitated, moved her feet and accidentally made contact.

The more the psychic talks, the more convinced I am that she's faking. She talks about Mama's son being at peace and in a happy place, which I guess the average family of a dead boy would find comfort in. But I am bitter disappointed at how she uses words so clever to trick people.

"There's something about a picture," the psychic says, "a special picture . . ."

Mama's hand goes to the photograph of me and "Max" she set down on the table when this whole less-than-worthless session began.

Well, of course that there picture is special, I think. *Why else would she of brought it?*

But the psychic says, "Not that one. A picture you have at home . . . from a special time . . . a happy time . . . Bubba says your son wants you to know . . . wants you to know . . . No, I'm sorry. It's gone now. Bubba is gone, he's wandered off. Sometimes spirits are fickle. And your son — he's not nearby. Sometimes that happens, too. We might have more success another time. I *do* consult by phone, you know."

This time I stomp on her foot for her barefaced attempt to get Mama to come back or to call, spending more money which she doesn't have to spare.

"Ow!" the psychic says.

"What's wrong?" Mama asks.

I don't know why the psychic doesn't accuse me, but she doesn't. "Cramp," she says. Then she says, "Healing wishes to you, honey. Remember that death is not the end, it's just another stop on the journey. And the love we bear for one another transcends all."

"Cheat!" I call her.

Ever so polite, Mama says, "Thank you," and she picks up the picture of me and Jeffrey-Max and goes home.

At home, she kind of wanders from room to room, looking at the pictures on the walls, obviously hunting for the one the psychic and Bubba were talking about.

My first inclination is to do nothing. "Mama!" I shout. "That psychic was a fake!"

But Mama's looking less tired, less haggard than she has in the last couple weeks.

Maybe all that happy nonsense the psychic spewed actually helped her.

I notice a picture on her desk, the one that was taken of me in sixth grade, right after that failed attempt to get my kite out of the tree. My arm is in a cast, but Mama and I are smiling, because the doctor had said I'd be fine. That was before the weird results came in from my blood work and we got called back in again. And then again. And then the doctor told her I had leukemia. It was before the chemo, and my losing my hair, and the first time I went to summer camp with the other cancer kids.

And, of course, it was way before I died two weeks ago.

But I give the picture a little shove so that it falls off the desk, and when Mama comes to pick it up, at first she's frowning, but then she says, "Heya, Cody."

I hate making that psychic look good, but Mama's first smile since I died is worth it.

YEAR
of the RAT

Danica Novgorodoff

December 31
Dear Nell,

Remember how last year we lined up the sparklers in your backyard and counted down to the new year? "Ten — BAM! — Nine — BAM! — Eight — BAM!" Time disappearing in a flash.

I can see it now — the seconds, minutes, hours, and days lined up in perfect, sparkling rows.

chk
chk
chk

My dear Nell,

Even here in these most strange, unusual places...

Not elected, of course, but highly popular among the upper, middle, and peasant class of citizenry in this prefecture. Well, What do you think of the show?
Miss, uh, Fishbowl is certainly—
A beauty, yes? My wife prefers I do not frequent the tent. You like a Chinese wife?
Well, I got a girl back home that—
Oh, but see, her shift is over. Very strict labor regulation in my town. Now it is time for the supreme prize attraction. You will see.
Some childrens found her in the tea fields outside a Dai village.
SQUEAK SQUEAK

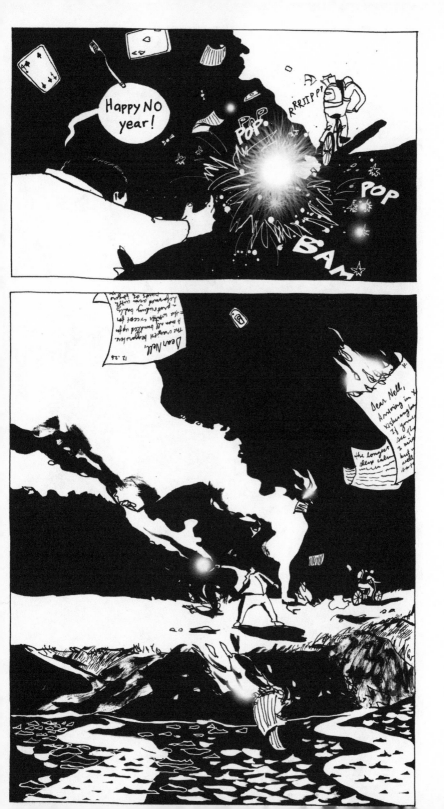

The Mummy's Daughter

ANNETTE CURTIS KLAUSE

My name is Tia Nafretiri. I am the daughter of a woman three thousand years old."

Tia undulated on stage to tinny Eastern music that crackled from a hidden Victrola. She was barely eighteen, if that, and a woman in the audience tittered.

Tia smiled. *The joke's on you,* she thought.

She danced in front of five vertical wooden sarcophagi, supposedly from the distant past, yet her sculpted black hair was very short in back and curved with the preciseness of a scimitar along her chiseled cheekbones in the extremely modern shingle bob that was all the rage in 1924. Tia understood why the woman doubted her.

Her silken bangs nearly touched her arching eyebrows, and the kohl outlining her eyes gave them a simmering

seductiveness. Those eyes made the men willing to sus-
pend disbelief, those and her full lips reddened with
oxblood lipstick. Tia knew this, and she teased them with
smoldering looks.

She was slight yet voluptuous. A beaded scarf criss-
crossed her hips snugly below her exposed belly, its fringe
falling to mid-thigh, and she wore a halter top stitched
with a wide collar necklace of turquoise and coral beads.
The men in the small audience, pressed tight as they
were around the tiny stage in the old boardwalk vari-
ety hall, were close enough to get a good eyeful of her.
Sometimes Tia had to avoid a grasp. She was tempted to
kick their hands, but didn't. After all, their desire meant
her act was working.

The women in the audience always looked more
skeptical, but Tia was used to disbelief. Even her fellow
show folk didn't believe her tale. That didn't bother her.
Everyone liked a good story. Any old floozy could get
up and dance the hootchy-kootchy for a bunch of rubes,
but the story made her act different.

"My mother lived in Egypt in the time of the pha-
raohs," Tia began as she rolled her hips to the whining
of exotic pipes. "She was a beautiful woman and a priest-
ess in the temple of Hathor. She honored the goddess by
dancing." Here Tia executed a turn and twined her arms
in the air like snakes as she made her finger cymbals ring
in time to the music. "When my mother danced, she
became the goddess on earth."

A man in the audience gave a short hoot that cut off abruptly, probably by the elbow of his girlfriend.

Tia stifled a chuckle. *Good for her,* she thought. "But my mother was forced by trickery to marry the evil high priest of Set," she said, and kept a straight face. "My dear mother had to give up dancing in the temple, and she lived in misery." Tia froze in place and snapped her head down as if bowed by sorrow. She held that pose for a moment. Martha said that she watched too many films, but Tia thought the move was very effective.

"Then a beautiful young man came to work for her husband to put in order his library." Tia swayed again to the softly sinuous music. "My mother could not take her eyes from him, and he could not stop looking at her.

"They became lovers."

Out of the corner of her eye, Tia saw Rueben Kiss, a dwarf boy with a curly tail poking out of the seat of his pants, scamper up to Martha Queen, the Giant Sword Swallower, who stood to the side of the stage. Martha had stolen Rueben from his parents when she was on the road with a small circus several years back, which sounded bad but wasn't because his parents had beaten and starved him. They didn't care enough to go after her. Tia adored Martha for that. Her father would have done the same thing. He was always taking in lost souls.

The little boy tugged Martha's dress, and the huge woman leaned down with an eager face to hear his tale. Why was he excited?

Tia tried to ignore them else she would lose the thread of her story, and she bent toward the audience as if imparting a secret.

"But the lovers were betrayed," Tia announced in a harsh whisper. "Her husband discovered them together."

Tia enjoyed hamming up this bit. Her voice rose with the drama.

"And her husband was insane!"

The music swelled, and hand drums pattered and throbbed with menace.

"He cut off her lover's head in front of her very eyes and dragged her to a waiting tomb. He paralyzed her with poison and stuffed her mouth with foul magic powders. He wrapped her in the linens of the dead and he said evil spells over her so that she would never die. He left her eyes uncovered, and she could see the coffin lid as he lowered it over her face—" Tia paused dramatically—"and he left her entombed alive for eternity."

The music cut off suddenly.

Tia rose, tall and rigid, onstage, her arms to her sides as if she were the one trapped in a sarcophagus, and she stood in silence for a count of six. She noted that even the doubting women in the crowd were now wide-eyed and captivated by her account.

"But the two great goddesses Isis and Hathor took pity on her," she continued finally. Soft plucked strings and the tapping *ching-ching* of the riqq, an Arabic tambourine, were audible in the background now, and Tia twirled twice, stamping her bare feet on the wooden planks of the stage very near the fingers of a young lounge lizard who was creeping them too near. He snatched his hand back. Tia pretended not to notice.

"The goddesses came to her in her torment and promised her she would be together with her love once more, for he would be reborn upon this earth and free her from her curse. They gave her the power to see beyond her tomb and her spirit the power to speak for her in dreams, so she would be ready when he came."

Tia noticed that Rueben and Martha had left. She wondered where they had gone, but she had a story to finish.

"Millennia passed," she told the audience as haunting pipes rejoined the strings.

"Then archeologists discovered my mother's tomb, and they brought her to this country.

"She stood for years in the study of a scholar, and though she could neither move nor speak, she could see and hear, so learned our language.

"Then one day a thrill ran through her." Tia shuddered and tinkled her finger cymbals, causing her beads and fringes to shimmy, much to the delight of the male audience members. "My mother felt him again. Her lover was reborn!"

Tia's radiant smile was spontaneous. It gave her pleasure to think of her father as part of the world.

"But before they could be reunited, she was stolen by

thieves and transported west as an exhibit in a cheap traveling show." Tia flung her right hand to the air in disgust.

"My mother used the power of dreams to lure her lover after her, though he knew not whom he sought." Tia rolled her hips in a seductive invitation. "He risked danger and death, but finally he found her. He used his wits and his flying knives to save her. And when, after so many centuries, he laid his hand on her again, the spell was broken and her eyes opened!"

Women in the audience sighed.

"They had nineteen wonderful years together. They trod the boards. She danced. She posed. He outlined her with knives. They gathered the greatest acts around them. They ran the most exciting show on earth. And she gave him a daughter—me."

Tia twirled and stamped and shimmied and celebrated her childhood, when she was surrounded by love. She stopped in the center of the stage.

"Then tragedy struck once more." Tia raised a hand to her eyes, and this time the sorrow she mimed was real.

A girl in the front row squeaked in protest, and Tia's heart warmed with a brief flush of gratitude.

"My father died of the Spanish flu in 1918," she told the audience as she hung her head and her hand flopped to her side. "My mother could not bear the loss." Tia found tears in her eyes despite herself. Not just for her father's death but for the way her mother had abandoned her. Didn't her mother think she was suffering, too? Wasn't that enough to make her stay? Didn't *she* matter?

"My mother decided to retreat to her sarcophagus and wait for him to be reborn once more."

There were murmurings in the crowd.

"You don't believe me?" she cried more forcefully than was needful. She strode to the central sarcophagus that stood upright at the back of the stage and yanked the wooden lid open. "There she waits!"

The audience gasped.

Inside stood a mummy, not wrapped but clad in a simple shift that revealed the dried-up wreckage of what was once a woman. Its brown, withered face was like crumpled leather polished here and there with wear. Yellow, cracked teeth peeked from between shriveled lips. Crooked stick-like fingers meshed in front of its abdomen. From one finger hung a ring with a turquoise stone, too large for the parchment-covered bone.

Does she still hear me? Tia wondered. *Can she see me as I tell her tale? How could she and be unmoved?*

"She is not gone entirely, however," Tia told the audience. "Her heritage lives on. As I grew up, my mother taught me how to dance—to dance how they did in the temples of ancient Egypt."

The music grew loud and quickened with the pulsing beat of drums.

"Get hot! Get hot!" yelled a young man in the audience, and his cronies laughed. *Idiot,* she thought.

As she whirled into her leaping, writhing, acrobatic finale, she saw the giantess at the back of the audience smothering Mrs. Ray, the owner of the show, in an embrace. No small woman herself, Mrs. Ray's gorgeous bearded face nearly disappeared into the bosom of Martha Queen. Mrs. Ray's father had been an undertaker, and she had inherited the dignified demeanor of his profession. Tia had to stop herself from laughing at the thought of the bearded lady spluttering with indignation at the effusive attentions of the giant woman. But why was Martha hugging her?

Tia soon had the opportunity to ask. As she exited the stage and stepped into her slippers, she found Martha back in the wings.

"What's happening, Mar?" Tia asked. "Why were you hugging the boss?"

"Oh, the poor dear," said Martha in a baritone whisper. "Her husband has run off."

Before Tia could ask more, the seven-and-a-half-foot woman dressed like the Statue of Liberty swept onstage, brandishing her swords.

Tia waved a thank-you to the stagehand who had manned the Victrola in back of the curtains, then she squeezed into the tiny room behind the stage. The building was one of a row of gingerbread wooden structures built along the boardwalk in the last century for the amusements. Backstage was old, creaky, and cramped, and always smelled of wet sand. She thanked the stars the show didn't have a fat lady. It was hard enough sharing close quarters with a giantess. A curtain for the performers' privacy hung ineffectively at one end of the room, but Tia preferred to throw a cloak over her costume and dash down the side road to her room in the boarding-house rather than change there. *Mrs. Ray should have someone build a proper partition,* she thought, not for the first time.

Rueben was perched on a stool, eating a hot dog, with his tail carefully curled over the edge of his seat. Lulu, the red-haired fire-eater, was dining with him, and also Tommy George, who was an all around blockhead, human ostrich, and swami—he could hammer nails up his nose, swallow and regurgitate live mice, and lie on a bed of nails while Martha split logs on his chest with an ax. Beside Tommy sat Jenny Flowers. She was the woman with four breasts—big ones on top, small ones below. She sang, badly, but no one seemed to care.

Tia had been with the show six months and had noticed that Mrs. Ray tended to surround herself with female performers, Tommy George excepted, but Tia suspected he was an Ethel. His act was manly, but his giggle was not.

"So, Mr. Ray beat it," Tia said to no one in particular as she settled on a rickety chair to join them.

"I don't know from nothin', kiddo," answered Jenny.

"She only cares about her double bubs," said Tommy.

Jenny punched him lightly, but she grinned and adjusted her strapless bras.

"He was a flat tire, anyway," Lulu added, and yawned, showing too much hot dog.

"I didn't think he was boring," Tia said. "He was a swell fella."

Lulu shook her head. "He was no good."

"Was you stuck on him, baby?" asked Jenny.

Tia laughed. "Lay off! You're all wet," she said. She had to admit he was useless even if he was good-natured. If she ran the show, she would have made him work for his living.

Rueben squirmed on his stool and wiped his mouth with a fist. "Nertz!" he exclaimed. "If she's gonna yell and be mean all the time, I'm hiding from her forever."

"Oh, she'll be Jake once she gets another man," said Lulu, patting the little boy's knee.

"This is the third feller that's run out on her," Jenny told Tia in a scandalized whisper.

"Three!" Tia gasped. Apparently the glossy black beard didn't stop Mrs. Ray from getting men, even if she couldn't keep them. "And only last night I heard her singing in the kitchen."

"That's funny since he's been gone two days," said Jenny.

"Maybe she sang to keep her spirits up," said Tia.

Lulu snorted. "Oh, yeah!"

They're a hard-boiled lot, Tia thought. Mrs. Ray wasn't a friendly woman, but everyone got equal stage time and was paid promptly. When Tia had come looking for a job, Mrs. Ray had been businesslike but generous. "I've been meaning to do something on an Egyptian theme," she had said. "I've already had some sarcophagi made. Your act will fit in perfectly." Tia had to admit that Mrs. Ray wasn't good with the day-to-day details of a show, however, and she rarely encouraged her troupe to excel. The performers deserved better.

"That was my last dance. I'm going home," Tia said, and grabbed her cloak from the back of her chair. "Lulu, I set your record by the Victrola, ready to go. Oh, and Tommy, there's some new nails in your kit."

"Jeepers creepers!" said Jenny. "What did we do before that girl?"

"You're a doll," said Tommy, standing up, too. He picked up his ax and the toolbox he stored beside it on a shelf in the back room. The toolbox contained a hammer and nails and miscellaneous other items he pierced his body with for the amusement of the audience.

Tia blushed. She was happy to do things for them. That was the way show folk should be with one another. Her father had always been clear about that.

She slipped out the back door into the alley, carefully peered in each direction to make sure no stage-door

Johnnies lingered, and was startled to discover two figures down near the dead end—and Mrs. Ray was one of
them. The other was a man in a swanky suit. He reached
out and nudged the strap of Mrs. Ray's long, slim evening
gown off her shoulder, and she chuckled. The moonlight
glinted on her carefully curled, dark beard and made it
look blue.

Tia stared. Mrs. Ray wasn't acting like a deserted
woman. Maybe the others were right to be cynical. She
shrugged off her disappointment and hurried up the
alley to a street that led away from the boardwalk.

Tia rattled open the front door to the clapboard
house owned by Mrs. Ray. The bearded lady lived on the
first floor and rented out the rooms on the second and
third floors. She had offered Tia lodgings right after she
had offered her the job. Some of the other boardwalk
performers stayed there, too. As Tia passed the entrance
to Mrs. Ray's rooms, a strange chemical odor assaulted
her nose. She wondered if the woman had taken up pho-
tography. The smells reminded her of those that had
wafted from her uncle Apollo's darkroom.

Upstairs in her stark little room, she changed into
a slim jersey two-piece that barely fell to her knees, and
then ate a cheese and pickle sandwich while she sat on
the edge of her bed. *Is this all there is for me?* she wondered. Her entire life she had been among show folk.
She had performed one way or another since she could

walk. Sometimes she wished she could try another career. She had money from her father's wise investments. She could buy a business, but what else was she prepared for? Nothing.

And now she had to look after that futzing mummy. In what other kind of life could she sit that in her parlor?

She was nervous about having to leave her mother's mummy down at the show, but there was no way she could drag it back here each night. She worried that the salt air was bad for it. That someone would try to steal it. That something bad would happen. Damn her mother for leaving her in charge. It wasn't fair.

Tia brushed her teeth and settled on her bed with her sewing bag and a needle and thread. Someone had to mend Rueben's pants. Martha loved him, but her fingers were too large for precise needlework, and Mrs. Ray hadn't tackled the problem. Sewing would occupy Tia's time until the show was over and she could go and check on the mummy, as she did every night. She sewed neat stitches and kept her eye on the clock on the mantelpiece. *Running a show wouldn't be bad,* she thought. *Dad did it really well. I'd rather be the captain than the crew. Someday,* she decided. This notion cheered her up.

After a while, she heard footsteps on the stairs and laughter. *Lulu's home,* she realized, *and she's got company. The show must be over.* She waited another thirty minutes to make sure everyone had left the theater. She didn't want the others to notice her concern. She didn't want anyone to suspect the mummy was any more than a prop, no matter what she told the audience.

Finally, she put her mending away and retrieved the key hidden under the clock. She had lifted the back-door key from Mrs. Ray's handbag while the bearded lady performed one afternoon, and had made a copy. She had felt ashamed for all of five seconds. The locksmith was on the next block, and she had brought the original key back in a jiffy. Now she could get into the theater anytime she wanted. She donned her T-strap heels and cloche hat and left.

The air outside was crisp and salty, and she could hear the gentle swoosh of the waves in the distance like applause far, far away—the applause from when she was little and had both parents.

She let herself in the theater's back door and used a small flashlight she had brought with her to make her way to the stage. There was no sense turning on the overhead light. Even though the few windows were all covered, a glow through the blinds might catch the eye of a cop on the beat. She propped the flashlight against the trim at the edge of the stage, and it lit the center sarcophagus with an inept beam—the central wavering brightness surrounded by a dim aureole. Darkness crowded in around the stage like an audience.

Tia removed the cover of the wooden sarcophagus and balanced it in the crook of her left arm so she could peer inside. No change. The mummy was as dark and crumpled and dry as ever.

"Oh, Mama," she whispered. "I miss you. Didn't you think a living, breathing Mama would have been a better comfort to me than this horrible inheritance?" She wiped a tear from her face with her fingers and touched the ring on the mummy's brown hand—her father's ring. After he died, her mother had hung his ring around her neck and wouldn't part from it even as she wasted away. Now it masqueraded as a paste prop in a boardwalk side-show.

Tia lowered her eyes in sorrow, and as she did, she noticed a patch of white on the floor.

Her brows knit. There was a trail of powder leading into the plywood sarcophagus to the right of her moth-er's solid wooden one. Tia carefully laid the lid she held down on the center of the stage and tried to open the other sarcophagus, but it was nailed shut.

She knelt and peered at the substance. Why would there be powder in the box?

Her thoughts flashed on lurid magazine stories of cocaine smugglers and white slavery. No, that couldn't be. Before she could help herself, she had dabbed a fin-ger in the mixture and brought it to her nose. There wasn't much of a smell to it. She touched her finger to the tip of her tongue.

The taste was saline and acrid. She spit it out.

All of a sudden, the chemical smell from Mrs. Ray's

rooms made sense. She scrambled to her feet, grabbed the flashlight, and ran to the back room to find Tommy's toolbox.

She brought the kit back and rummaged for what she needed. Under the hammer and amid the awls and nails she found a sturdy screwdriver. She used it to pry up the plywood lid. This took longer than she had thought, and her hands trembled with nerves so much that the screwdriver slid and gashed her left palm. She snatched her hand away, sending droplets of blood across the mummy, and she cursed.

She wrenched the lid back and it came away, splintering slightly.

Out drifted the same chemical odor she had smelled outside Mrs. Ray's door. The same chemical odor she now recognized from when the man had come to embalm her father with his portable pump and bottles of formaldehyde.

And inside the sarcophagus slumped a body.

Its face was pale and bloodless, its eyes closed, and its lips sewn together, but she recognized Mr. Ray.

Tia backed away in shock, the lid clutched to her chest. Mrs. Ray had learned more than her dignified demeanor from her father, it seemed. Was she embalming as she sang in her kitchen last night?

But this wasn't a corpse for an open casket viewing, and that must be why she had stuffed the body with washing soda, baking soda, and salt—the modern equivalent of the natron that the ancient Egyptians had used to create mummies.

Tia shivered. The woman was insane. A mummy would take years to cure properly, and all the while Mrs. Ray would have to keep it hidden.

She looked askance at the other sarcophagi. Were there other mummies? Other husbands had disappeared, hadn't they?

Tia set to work, screwdriver and hammer in hand. Now that she had the hang of it, the work went quicker, and one lid after another came off.

Finally, she stood in front of a grisly display. Flanking the female mummy to either side, like macabre chorus boys, were four male mummies in various stages of completion.

"What do I do now?" Tia wondered aloud.

"Put the lids back on, if you please," uttered a cold voice.

Tia's heart leaped to her throat, and she whirled toward the speaker. The bearded lady stood stage right with Tommy George's ax raised in her hands. Her eyes blazed with anger, and her knuckles were white with her grip.

"What are you doing here?" Tia gasped.

"Why, I came to tuck my husbands into bed," said Mrs. Ray, and choked off a bitter laugh.

Tia eyed the ax warily. If she could keep the woman talking, maybe she could figure out what to do.

"You've had three husbands, haven't you? Who is the fourth man?"

"My father," answered Mrs. Ray. She stepped forward and briefly let go of the ax with one hand to stroke the sarcophagus nearest her.

Tia edged backward.

"He wanted me to take over in the embalming room, where no one would see my affliction," said Mrs. Ray. "Then he discovered he could make more money off me in the entertainment business," she sneered. "He had his entertainment from me, too." Hurt twisted her face at the memory, and Tia didn't want to imagine what had happened but couldn't help it.

"Men are evil," said Mrs. Ray. "They make us feel things, filthy things, shameful things. They prey upon our weakness. They must be punished."

Tia glanced to where she'd left the toolbox, next to her flashlight at the edge of the stage. She had an idea.

Mrs. Ray's eyes narrowed. "And naughty girls must be punished, too," she growled.

"Leave her be!" a woman's rough, hollow voice cried out.

Mrs. Ray looked around her wildly, swinging the ax in front of her.

Whoever had come to help might need rescuing as much as she did. Tia made a dash for the front of the stage, fell to her knees, snatched up the toolbox, and rolled off the edge into the shadows.

But then she was startled to hear Mrs. Ray laugh. "There's no one there! So, you have talents as a ventriloquist, you sly cat. I'll cure you of that."

She ran toward Tia with the ax over her head, and just as she bent her knees to jump, Tia rose up and hurled three awls from the toolbox at her.

They didn't fly as straight as a knife would. One missed, one stuck in Mrs. Ray's arm, and the last struck her square in the breast.

The bearded lady screamed and dropped the ax to clutch her chest.

"No, I can't throw my voice," Tia told her, "but my father taught me how to throw knives."

Where *had* the voice come from? Would someone help?

Mrs. Ray dashed Tia's momentary hope when she crouched and took up the ax again.

Tia rummaged in the toolbox for another weapon. Would a screwdriver pierce flesh? The front door was chained. Could she dodge past the crazy bearded lady and escape out the back?

Then a shadow appeared behind Mrs. Ray. A skeletal hand grasped the bearded lady's arm.

"Leave my daughter alone!"

"Mama!" Tia sobbed.

Mrs. Ray turned. The ax fell from her hands once more and clattered to the floor. She shrieked and shrieked and shrieked—then ran.

In the distance, the back door slammed.

Tia clambered back onto the stage and embraced the small, bony figure more wraith than human.

"Your arms are like the coils of Sed Em Ra," said the mummy. "Within them is the ordered world, and outside his coils lay chaos."

"What brought you back?" Tia asked, releasing her grip lest she damage the fragile figure.

"Your tears and your blood brought me back," said the mummy. Already her face grew softer, her lips fuller. "I should have never left. I was blinded by sorrow."

Although she still trembled, Tia was surprised to find she was amused. "You chose a good moment."

"Indeed," answered the mummy, "but I believe you would have triumphed nevertheless. You are strong, like your father. I am proud of you."

Her mother's words made Tia glow. Had she been strong the whole time and not known it? She had made her way in the world alone and survived, that was sure. Now she didn't have to.

"What will we do now?" Tia asked her mother.

"I believe there is a show without a mistress," said the mummy, "so run the show."

Tia hesitated, surprised by her mother's words. Run the show? "Sorry," she said in response to her mother's expectant look. "My brain is still on 'don't get axed by the crazy woman.'"

"You can do it. You know you can," said the mummy,

and she stroked her daughter's cheek with elegant fingers. "I'll help. I promise."

Tia knew she was grinning like a fool. She could do it, she thought. She really could do it. The realization was like fresh sweet air filling her lungs. Her gaze swept the dimly lit theater with pride, then fell on the mummified husbands once more.

"First I'd better call the cops."

When God Came to Kathleen's Garden

DAVID ALMOND

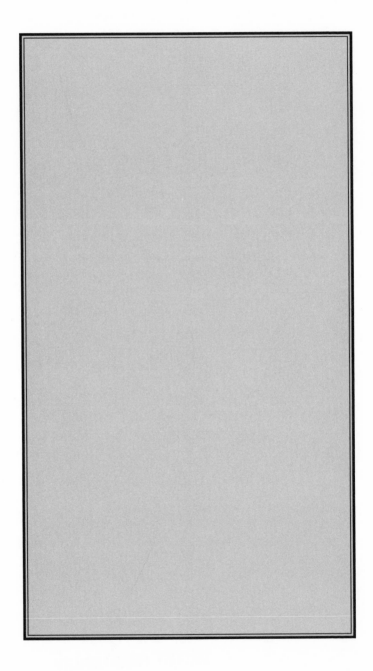

A Tuesday morning, late August. Sun blazing down but I was pretty fed up. I'd packed a sack with sandwiches and soda and crisps. I had my photograph albums and autograph albums and pens. I was supposed to be going to Newcastle with Tex Flynn. The plan was we'd watch the United players training and get some autographs. In those days you could wander about on the training ground with them. You could jog with them through the streets. They were brilliant and famous. They played in front of thirty thousand fans every week, but there they were, right beside us. They played keep up, head tennis, penalties, shots. They were always laughing and playing daft tricks on one another, but suddenly one of them would do something that seemed impossible. Sometimes they'd let us join in. They'd fall down when we dribbled past them; they'd dive the wrong way when we took penalties. They'd pretend to be amazed by our tricks, to be terrified by the power of our shots. They didn't keep the magic to themselves. One day Alan Suddick showed me how to swerve the ball with the outside of my foot. Dave Hilley told me it wasn't power that made a great shot, it was timing. He spent ten minutes or more with me, passing the ball to me, telling me to fire it back. "That's good, son," he said. "You'll get there. Practice, practice, practice, till you're doing it without a thought." Lots of lads went, especially in the summer holidays, when the team was getting in shape for the new season. We all had autograph books and albums packed with photos we'd cut out of the papers. The players were great. They all signed our books. *Best wishes,* they wrote, or *Keep on kicking* or *Have a great life!*

But on that very day, Tex had gone down with flu, which seemed pretty weird at that time of year.

"Are you sure?" I asked his mam when she answered the door with the news.

"Of course I'm sure," she said. "He woke up in a dreadful state. I'd let you go up and see him, but you don't want to catch it yourself, do you?"

I looked past her into the shadowy hall, towards the stairs going up to his bedroom. I thought of his room. It was just like mine: black-and-white stripes everywhere, stacks of old football programmes in cardboard boxes, photographs of the heroes pinned to the walls. I thought of him lying there, sweating and shivering and taking Beecham's Powders and drinking orange juice and sniffing Vicks.

She shrugged.

"I'm sorry, Davie," she said. "Is there anybody else you could go with?"

I thought about it, but there was nobody. Nobody else loved the team as much as Tex and I did.

I just stood and stared at her. The sack was heavy on my back. She smiled sweetly.

"Never mind," she said. "You go back home, son. I'm sure he'll be better in a few days time, and then you can have a lovely day out together."

She smiled again, said good-bye, and shut the door.

I walked back home up Felling Bank. I started to run, like always. I kicked a pebble. I dribbled it around the lampposts and telegraph poles. I heard the crowd all around me, yelling me on. I heard them singing "Blaydon Races." In my head, I said, *He's beaten one man! He's beaten two! Can he do it? Can he?* I sidestepped a little dog that came out of nowhere. I dashed forward, dropped my shoulder, swerved one way then the other, and flicked the pebble through an open gate. I punched the air. I raised my arms to the sky. "Yes! Yeeeees! What a goal!" And the dog danced and yapped around me.

Back at home, in the garden, I sat on the back step.

I told my mam about Tex, and she just said all the things that Tex's mam had said.

I looked up at the blazing sun and the clear blue sky.

"But how can he get flu in *August*?" I said.

"Because he *can*. It happens to lots of people. And if you think about it—instead of just thinking about yourself for once—it's the worst of all times to catch it, when the weather's so hot. It must be awful for the poor lad."

She folded her arms and looked down at me.

"Now, I hope you're not going to sit moping all day."

I got one of my albums out. I'd just stuck some new pictures in. There was a brilliant one from the *Pink:* Dave lashing in the winner against Swansea City under the headline HILLEY SINKS THE SWANS. There was an even better one of Alan. He was horizontal, four feet off the ground. His eyes were bright with concentration. The ball had just left his head and was on its way to the goal. His arms were spread wide, just like he was flying. Alan Suddick. Dave Hilley. There was nobody like them. They could do anything.

I played with the biro I'd bought specially for today. I clicked the tip in and out. I dreamed I was a famous player. I imagined lots of kids lining up in front of me. I scribbled my name fast on scraps of paper.

"That's OK, son," I murmured. "It's a pleasure, lad."

I drank my soda. I chewed my sandwiches. I crunched the crisps. I thought of all the lads that'd be at the training ground. I thought of Tex in his bed. Maybe he was

just putting it on. Maybe he was going off the team.
Maybe he was going off *me*.

Voices kept echoing across the roofs from the playing fields outside the estate.

"On me head! On me head!"

"Get stuck in!"

"Man on!"

"Goal! Goal! Yeeeeees!"

Mam watched me through the kitchen window. She
came out again.

"You're wasting a beautiful summer's day," she said.
"There's a million things you could do instead of sitting
there and staring into space."

"A million?" I said.

"Yes."

"Like what?"

"You could go and play football with the lads. You
could cut that grass, instead of letting it grow around you
like a jungle."

"That's two things," I said.

She clicked her tongue. She glared at me.

"You watch your lip," she said. "One thing you could
certainly do is stop staring at those daft pictures. There's
nothing special about those fellers. They're just people,
just like you."

She went back in. I turned my back on her. What did
she mean "just like me?" She hadn't seen Dave Hilley
dribble. She hadn't seen Alan Suddick make a free kick.

These "fellers" could work miracles! I closed my eyes.
I tried to feel like Alan when he smashed the ball into
the net. I tried to feel like Dave when he left a defender
sprawling in the dirt. I practised Dave's signature until it
was just like his. I wrote *To Davie. Best wishes, Dave Hilley*
on his picture.

"Thanks, Dave," I said.

I said, "You're welcome, son," in Dave's gentle Scottish
accent.

I signed Alan's picture. *To Davie, a true fan. Yours in
sport. Alan Suddick.*

I grinned and winked like Alan did.

"No bother, lad," I whispered.

I sat there, in the sunshine, in the dream.

Then there were footsteps behind me. Two of my sisters, Mary and Margaret, were there.

"What do *you* want?" I grunted.

Mary put her finger to her lips.

"Shh," she said.

Mam waved at them through the kitchen window.
They waved back.

"It's a *secret*," Margaret whispered.

I sighed.

"What is?"

They looked at each other. They turned so that Mam
couldn't see their faces.

"God's come," said Mary.

"What?" I said.

"God's come. He's in Kathleen Kelly's garden," said Mary. "He was fast asleep and now he's woke up and he's sitting under the cherry tree. Are you coming to see? Kathleen said you should, but nobody else."

I rolled my eyes. What a pair.

"Please," said Margaret. "And hurry up, before he goes away."

I sighed again. I looked at Mam. She'd have me cutting the grass if I didn't do something soon. So I stood up. I still had my album and my biro in my hand. Mam waved as we headed out.

We went out the gate and headed down the street towards Kathleen's.

"How do you know it's God?" I said.

"Kathleen says it must be," said Mary. "She said she's been saying loads of prayers since Jasper died. She's been begging him to help her. And he's sitting just where Jasper's buried."

"And he looks *just* like his pictures," said Margaret.

"And he appeared like magic," said Mary. "Out of nothing."

"So it's true," said Margaret. "Isn't it?"

I said nothing. How did *I* know?

We went into Kathleen's front gate and down the side of her house and into the back garden. Kathleen was kneeling on the lawn beside the little fishpond with her hands joined. Mary and Margaret knelt down beside her and joined their hands, too, like they were in church.

Mary looked at me like she thought I should kneel down as well, but I didn't.

God was sitting with his back against the trunk of the cherry tree. The sun was shining down on him through the leaves.

"This is Davie, Lord," said Kathleen.

God looked at me and smiled.

He had dark skin and dark eyes. He wore loose orange robes and brown sandals. He was bald and he had a pot-belly and a big white beard.

He raised a hand in greeting. I nodded at him.

"Do your mam and dad know?" I asked Kathleen.

She shook her head.

"Dad's at work," she said. "Mam's doing the shopping."

"Does he talk?" I said.

"We don't know."

God smiled. He picked a stone up from the edge of the pond. He showed it in his hand, closed his hand, then opened it again and the stone had gone. Then he took the same stone out of his left ear and put it back by the pond again. Margaret clapped. God snapped a stick and put it back together again. He took another stick as long as his arm and opened his mouth and swallowed it and drew it out again.

He smiled and giggled, and the girls clapped.

I saw tears in Kathleen's eyes.

She clasped her hands tight and leaned right towards God.

"Please, Lord," she said.

He turned his face towards her. She chewed her lips.

"I see your powers, Lord," she whispered. "Please, Lord, could you possibly bring Jasper back to us?"

God smiled. He reached up, plucked something from the empty air, then showed a handful of silver coins to us. He dropped them into Margaret's hands.

"Please," Kathleen begged. "Please. I know you can."

He plucked a bird's egg from the air. He tossed it up, and a little bird flew away singing. He smiled at Kathleen. He rested his hands on his potbelly. He leaned back against the tree. He stretched and yawned.

The air was so warm, so still. There was a gate at the back of Kathleen's garden that led to a park and then to the playing fields. There were kids yelling out there. There were mad cries from the lads as a goal was scored.

"Yes! It's in! Yeeeees!"

I looked at God and knew he wasn't God. His clothes were dusty and worn. His sandals were tied together with string. His face was filthy. He looked like he'd walked miles. He was just some weird bloke who'd wandered in for a nap in the shade. He must have come in from the park or somewhere.

So stupid. I should have gone and played football. I should have gone to Newcastle on my own.

"We should tell somebody about him," I said.

"But who?" said Mary.

"Father O'Mahoney?" said Margaret. "Or the pope, maybe?"

"No!" said Kathleen. "He came to my garden. He came just for us. Can you, Lord? Please, Lord. Please bring Jasper back."

It was hopeless. I was stuck. I couldn't just clear off and leave them here with him.

"When's your mam coming back?" I said to Kathleen.

She just shook her head and kept on staring at God.

God put his hand into the pond. He smiled down at the goldfish flickering there. He took his hand out and let water trickle from his hand across his brow. Kathleen reached out. She caught some drops and touched them to her own brow. God smiled at her. He opened his mouth, took three goldfish out, and slid them gently down into the water.

"Will you sign my book?" I asked.

I showed it to him. God raised his eyebrows.

"They're all footballers in here," I said. "They play for Newcastle. But there's an empty page you could use."

I knelt down and shuffled nearer to him. He smelt spicy and sweet, like the cinnamon Mam put on the top of rice pudding.

I opened the book, and God's eyes widened.

"They're footballers," I said.

God laughed softly. He pointed to Alan Suddick.

"Yes, that's Alan Suddick, God," I said. "He's brilliant! And so's Dave Hilley. Look, that's him scoring the winner against Swansea."

God nodded. He ran his fingers over Alan's face, over Dave's face. He smiled as if he knew them well.

I showed him where it said, *To Davie. Best wishes, Dave Hilley.*

"That's how the footballers do it," I said. "Will you write that? And will you sign it from God."

I held out the new biro, and he took it. He played with it for a moment, smiling as he clicked the point in and out and in and out. He held it to his ear to listen to the clicks. His fingers seemed very gentle. He ran them across the empty page as if he loved the feel of it. Then he licked his lips and started to copy: *To Davie. Best wishes.* He concentrated hard, but he couldn't hold the pen properly, and his writing was all uneven and clumsy. He looked at what he'd written. It looked like:

7o Douic. 13es4 iiil5Hes.

He sighed and shrugged as if to say he was sorry but it was the best he could do.

"That's great, Lord," I said. "Thank you. Will you put your name now, please?"

He put the pen on the page again. I held his hand this time. It was soft and warm. I guided him as he wrote, *God.*

I read the words out loud. God giggled. I giggled with him.

"Now you're there in the book with Alan and Dave," I said.

Kathleen was furious. She glared at me. She glared at Mary and Margaret.

"I hope you two aren't going to ask for something now!" she whispered. "This is *my* garden!"

Mary and Margaret shook their heads.

"Good!" said Kathleen. "Please, God. *Please!*"

I sighed. I looked at my album. She might as well ask Alan or Dave to bring her dog back. I looked at a photo of Alan leaping over a clumsy defender. I looked at Dave balancing the ball on his knee. I closed my eyes. I imagined kneeling before them on the training ground. *Please, Alan. Please, Dave. Please bring Jasper back again.*

I thought of Jasper, the way he used to run around. He was an ordinary little black-and-white dog. A jumpy, yappy, happy thing, part spaniel, part poodle, part something else. He'd come from a big litter from somewhere on Brettanby Road. He was just a few years old, too young to die, but some disease got into him and there was no saving him. Mr. Watkinson, the vet in Felling Square, had put the poor thing down. I'd seen Kathleen and her mam bringing Jasper back in a brown shopping bag. Mary and Margaret had seen Kathleen's dad digging his grave. Sometimes at night I thought of him lying down there in the dark, his little body turning to dust, to earth. Now I thought of the earth reforming itself, becoming Jasper again. So stupid.

God smiled at Kathleen. There was great kindness

in his eyes. He lifted himself from the grass. He stood up and rubbed his knees and his back as if they were aching. He stretched and yawned. He stroked his beard like he was wondering about something, then he put his hand deep into his robes and took out a little box. There was a picture of a beautiful faraway mountainous place on it. He opened it, and there were sweets inside. He held them out to us. They were delicious, soft and mysteriously sweet and dusted with the finest sugar.

We chewed and sighed and licked our lips at their deliciousness.

"They're lovely, God!" said Mary.

He smiled and put the whole box into her hands. Then he shrugged and raised his hand as if in farewell.

"But where are you going?" asked Kathleen.

"Aaaaah," said God.

It was the first thing we'd heard him say.

"And what about Jasper?" asked Kathleen.

"Aaaaaah," he said again, but much more sadly.

Kathleen jabbed her finger towards the earth.

"He's down there in the ground!" she said. "And I've been praying to you and praying to you and praying to you!"

God looked down at the earth beneath the cherry tree. He spread his hands and closed his eyes. He sighed. He reached out to Kathleen and squeezed her gently on the shoulder, then he just turned and walked towards the gate into the park.

We watched him walking away. He walked slowly and easily, rocking gently from side to side. He walked across the playing fields. Children ran to him. He kept reaching into his robes, taking things out, giving them to the children.

Kathleen stamped her foot.

"See? Everybody gets something!" she said. "You get silver coins, you get sweets, you get his autograph, they get what he's giving them. And what do I get? Absolutely nothing!"

She yelled after God.

"What about Jasper? What about my dog, *Jasper*?"

God didn't turn.

"You don't care!" she yelled. "I don't believe in you!"

He hesitated, but he didn't turn.

Kathleen stamped the ground, then realised she was stamping right on top of Jasper. It just made her cry some more.

"Oh!" she yelled. "Why don't all you silly people just go home?"

But we didn't go. We stayed in the garden. We shared the sweets. I looked at the pictures of Alan and Dave, and I wished I had a picture of God to go with his autograph.

After a while I said, "It wasn't really God, you know."

Kathleen stamped her feet again. She raised her fists in the air.

"I know that!" she said. "Do you think I don't know *that*?"

I kept thinking I should go, but I didn't go. I wondered about Tex and his flu. *I bet he's had a miraculous recovery,* I thought. *I bet he's out playing football right now.*

I heard Margaret whispering to Mary.

"Was it not God, Mary?"

Mary shook her head.

"No. Of course not. Shh."

We sat sadly in silence.

Soon, Kathleen's mam came home. She was loaded down with shopping bags.

"Hello, everybody," she said. "And Davie as well! Hello, stranger."

She brought a packet of custard creams out and handed them around. She dug into her handbag and took out a leaflet.

"The town's full of funny folk giving these out," she said. "Look what's coming to town."

A circus. There was a picture of a big top, a pony, a tiger, a girl swinging on a trapeze.

And on the back there it was, a picture of God in his orange robes and sandals and with his great white beard.

THE MISTERIOUS SWAMI, it said, THE GREAT ORIENTAL MAGICIAN. SEE SWAMI, AND YOU WILL BELEIVE IN MIRACLES!

Margaret gasped. Kathleen put her tongue out at me. She flicked some crumbs from her lips. I was already imagining the picture stuck in my book close to the pictures of Dave and Alan. Maybe I could find Swami again and get him to sign it with his real name.

"Is everything all right, love?" said Mrs. Kelly to Kathleen.

"Yes!" snapped Kathleen.

Mrs. Kelly smiled. She put her arm around Kathleen.

"Oh, love," she said softly. "Jasper loved you very much, you know."

Kathleen cried. Mrs. Kelly looked me in the eye, and I knew she wanted us to go.

"Come on," I said to my sisters, and we all got up.

We were heading down by the side of the house when the barking started.

"What's that?" said Mary.

"It's Jasper!" gasped Margaret.

"Don't be silly!" I said.

But we all looked back. The barking came from the other side of the gate into the park. We could hear paws scratching and scratching there. We could hear the dog flinging itself against the gate. We stepped back into the garden.

"Somebody sounds very excited," said Mrs. Kelly.

The dog barked and yapped and yelped.

"Go away!" she said, but it barked and barked.

"Do we dare to let it in?" she said.

Margaret clasped her hands together. She closed her eyes tight and tilted her face towards the sky.

"I'll go," said Kathleen at last. "I'm the one that's good with dogs, aren't I?"

She wiped the tears from her eyes with her sleeve. She went to the gate. She stood on tiptoes and looked over it.

"Oh!" she cried.

She looked back at us with amazement in her eyes. Then turned to the dog again.

"Oh, welcome home!" she cried.

And she opened the gate, and the little yappy black-and-white dog raced in.

影團

THE SHADOW TROUPE

Shawn Cheng

(Hou Yi, the legendary archer, saved the world by shooting down all but one of the ten Suns that were scorching the Earth.)

(Hou Yi was granted the Elixir of Life and entrusted it to Chang'e, his wife. The covetous Peng Meng schemed to take the Elixir by force.)

(Hou Yi killed the traitor, but it was too late. Chang'e swallowed the Elixir and floated to the Moon, where she remains to this day.)

(According to legend, the Jade Hare lives on the Moon and grinds medicine for the gods.)

Cat Calls

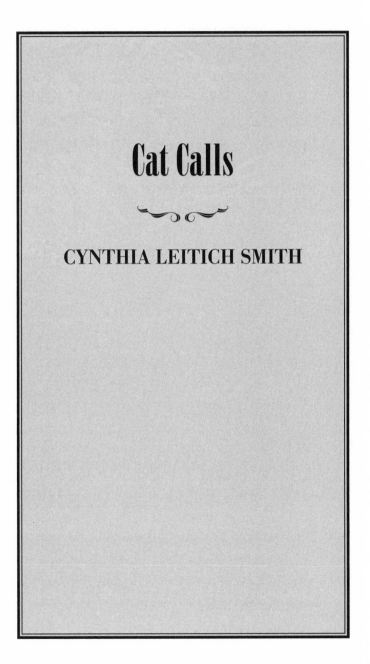

CYNTHIA LEITICH SMITH

H ey, Tiff, how 'bout a *man* in your future?" Aiden calls from the nearest concession stand as he pours butter-flavored oil into the popcorn popper.

The scent of rotating sausages and heating cheese makes my stomach rumble, but I yawn and hurry on my catty-corner path across the main drag toward my grand-mother's tent. What with working nights, I can't seem to get enough sleep anymore. I spent this afternoon on the living lot crashed on a hammock in the sunshine.

The carnival scene is only vaguely freakish. Sure, talk has it that the carousel is haunted and my grandma really has the sight and the owner is some kind of shape-shifter, but that's just talk. And our roustabouts are on the tough side, but you could say the same for the losers back at my high school in Detroit. Other than one bit-off ear and one small-time drug bust, nothing remotely interesting has happened all summer.

Right now, we're set up on the outskirts of Nowhere, Oklahoma. It's July, just past sundown, and the front gates open in fifteen minutes. It's also ungodly hot, dry from the drought, and pink clay dust is blowing everywhere.

As I saunter on, exaggerated kissing sounds trail me from the ex-con taking position at the Ferris wheel. A low whistle emerges from his brother-in-law, who's touching up the red paint on the barred wagon labeled MAN-EATING SNAKE.

Alongside a tin-can-alley game, I glimpse white teeth, the shadowy profile of a lean cowboy. A stranger. As I pause for a better look, he's gone.

Still, I stretch my arms over my head and arch my back, just to give the rest of the boys something to look at, showing off how my orange baby-doll T and denim cutoffs accent my curves. I'm a flirt, I admit it. I love the attention, especially 'cause it's so new.

I'm what people call "a late bloomer." This May, not long after my sixteenth birthday, I finally started my period for the first time and shifted from blah to bomb-shell overnight.

For me, it was a relief. My mom, on the other hand, had a full-scale panic attack. Before you could say "Xanax," she packed me up and shipped me off to my grandmother, who at the time was predicting the future in Missouri off I-35.

I tilt my head at one last whistle as I enter Granny Z.'s tent.

"Cat calls," she mutters, glancing up from the table where she's filing her long nails. "You're late."

I find Granny fascinating. She's a tightly built woman, with golden-brown hair like mine, turned rusty from the dust. She goes by "Madame Zelda," pretends like she can read my mind, and looks anywhere from age seventy to a hundred and ten.

As I wiggle out of the T and shorts, Granny strolls over to hand me a loose-fitting, gauzy dress. It's black and lavender with sheer, draping sleeves, silver sequins, and long fringe. Matching funky scarves drape from a beat-up freestanding coat hanger in the corner. The rest of the tent is the fortune-teller's stage.

My grandmother honestly believes in crystallomancy and claims "psychic ability is common among the women of our line." It's no big deal. She's a little nutty, but who isn't? I've been amazed by how many people believe in this crap.

Tonight will be my first behind the ball. It was Granny Z.'s idea, apparently inspired by the one time back in June when she tried to read my future in the crystal. Granny claimed I'd someday join in the family tradition, and said she'd let me know when the time was right.

At first, it sounded kind of fun, playing the fortune-teller, like dressing up on Halloween. So far as I can tell, it's mostly a matter of watching your marks for clues and telling them what they want to hear.

That sounds easy enough in theory. But here, tonight, moments away from facing real live people, the whole thing suddenly feels a lot more complicated. What if I totally blank? Or the marks get pissed at me for being such a lame and obvious faker?

"I'm not sure I can do this," I admit, though I'd hate to let her down.

"You?" Granny smoothes my long hair and tucks a strand behind my ear. "Who knows what you can do? You don't even know yet."

She's always saying things like that. Occupational hazard, I suppose.

"I'm off now," she adds. "See you at breakfast!"

"What?" I put my hand on her forearm. "Wait. You're leaving me here? Alone?"

Moving away, she says, "I'm leaving you to your future."

"Are you kidding?" What is she thinking? I can't believe it! I mean, OK, yes, she does mysteriously disappear overnight sometimes. I'm sort of getting used to that. But what could be so important tonight? "What if something goes wrong?"

Ignoring my protests, Granny Z. continues on her way, and I wonder for the first time if she might have a boyfriend. She's quite the vixen for a grandma, and I see her playing cards sometimes with the old alligator man.

Granny is my father's mother. He died on I-96 when his Harley-Davidson was sideswiped by a Greyhound bus. I wasn't even born yet.

According to Mom, I was the product of an adolescent hookup at some house party in Ypsilanti, Michigan, involving vodka, a speedboat, and a Pink Floyd album. Dad died two days later, before they knew about me or even had a chance to really talk.

Granny Z. showed up for the first time, unannounced, at our front door when I was ten. She inspected me like I was competition livestock, cooked pork chops for dinner, and after I went to bed she spent all night whispering with my mother in the kitchen.

Granny left after pancakes the next morning and never visited again. Once in a while, though, Mom would mention that Granny called her at work. I didn't get any phone calls, but Granny did send me cards, each with a dollar in it, on my birthdays.

I thought this summer would be my chance to get to know her, to finally learn more about my father. I underestimated the hell out of how tight-lipped the old lady can be.

Granny Z. uses a palm-sized crystal ball for her own purposes, but she breaks out the seven-inch diameter one for professional readings. The large quartz is exquisite, flawless, sits on a matching stand, and is so heavy that I need both hands to lift it.

The ball, the outfits, the ambience . . . like in the movies, Granny says. It sells.

I tie a long scarf around my hair, light the votive candles and cypress incense, and set a short stack of business cards on the black tablecloth.

If I'm going to pull this off, I've got to get into the spirit, so to speak, or at least manage a halfway decent job of acting the part. Taking deep breaths, I try to do as Granny Z. instructed me. I gaze into the crystal, trying to unfocus my vision, trying to imagine myself in a room of white light, trying to feel any vibrations.

By the time my first customers arrive, I've still failed to convince myself that the mist rising within the ball has some mystical source. I'm positive it's just a product of the humidity and shadows.

I lean out of the tent and smile at the fire juggler across the way. He raises his eyebrows suggestively, and I resist the urge to smirk.

Instead, I use one finger to beckon a couple of townie girls to join me inside. They grab each other's hands, giggling, and I cover my growling stomach with my hand.

We don't ask for money up front. The sign reads:

MADAME ZELDA

SPIRITUAL CONSULTANT

FIRST TWO MINUTES FREE

The two minutes is my window. If I can reel in the marks, they'll pay a buck for each additional two.

I pull up an extra chair from the side of the tent, and the girls elbow each other playfully as they settle in. Usually it's better to field "clients" one at a time (they're less sure of themselves that way), but I took one look at these two and knew I'd lose both if I tried to separate them.

They're about my age, probably a little older, which doesn't help my credibility.

I'm grateful for the dark, the flickering candlelight.

Hoping they haven't caught a good look at me, I snatch an additional gauzy scarf, drape it over my head, and bring the sides down to cover more of my face.

Then I study the girls. Obviously, they're from the local small town. They feel safe enough in their world to wear real gold jewelry to a carnival. One set of earrings is heart-shaped, the other clover-shaped. Their thin rope necklace-and-bracelet sets look alike. Their matching hairstyle is about three years ago. Clear fingernail polish, no tats, no extra piercings, easy on the makeup, wardrobe by Wal-Mart. They're good girls, middle class, possibly honor roll, probably churchgoing, and definitely best buds.

From their breath, I can tell that they both had corn dogs and onion rings with lemonades for dinner. Walking into my tent is about as close as they come to having a wild side.

I poise my elbows on the table and place my finger-tips beneath my chin.

"What would you have me ask the ball?" I'm using a voice I practiced earlier. It's lower and breathier than my regular one.

The girls exchange glances. Then the one with the heart earrings nudges her friend. "Ash, ask her about—"

"Shut up!" is the answering exclamation. The blush that goes with it is clue one.

I show my palms. "I must have quiet."

It's important that I stay in control. I inhale deeply again and again.

I don't see anything in the ball, except maybe my own reflection. It's my fault, a rookie mistake—since I shut the tent flap, the flames have been burning steadily. I've got no flickers, no shadows or intriguing shapes to report.

"I see a boy," I claim. "Or is it a young man?" Obviously, that's want they want to hear. That's what most girls want to hear. "I, um, I see a heart and a . . . clover."

Sweat trickles down my spine.

Before they make the connection between my read-ing and their accessories, I nod to Ash. "I see you with a young man in . . ." In? *In?* Scrambling to tie it together, I conclude, "A field of clover! He's your great love."

Their eyes go wide, and Ash bites her lower lip.

"I may be able to tell you more, but the mists are dis-sipating. For only a dollar—"

Ash's laugh turns from a giggle to a bark. "I don't

think so." She reaches for her friend's—no, I realize—her *girlfriend's* hand. "Wow, do you suck at this!"

As they jump up to leave, I call, "Wait, the signs can have many meanings!"

The couple drops hands before exiting the tent, but neither one glances back.

Well. Ash was right. I do suck at this.

God, it's not even 8:00 p.m. yet. I'm looking at a long night.

Before I can worry too much, a middle-aged lady sticks her head in. "Is it my turn? I don't mean to press, but if anyone tells my husband I'm—"

"Come in." It doesn't matter whether she's embarrassed about seeing a fortune-teller or that her husband will think we're both acolytes of the dark powers. I'm eager to do better this time.

I move briefly to the rear of the tent and prop the back flap open with the extra chair to let in the warm breeze. At least the flames will be moving. "Sit."

She practically scurries into the chair. I'd guess she's in her early- to mid fifties, about forty pounds overweight. She colors her short hair a dark brown, and she's wearing a faded denim jumper with an embroidered ladybug design over a short-sleeved white T-shirt. The smile lines around her eyes are deep, but so are the worry ones above her eyebrows. It's all I can do not to choke on the smell of her hair spray and floral perfume.

"My name is Brenda," she says.

"Welcome," I reply in my stage voice. "What would you have me ask the ball?"

Her hand goes to a silver cross hanging from her necklace. "My son . . ."

"You're worried about him?"

She nods. "His job is dangerous."

I'm thinking he's military, police, fire, or maybe in high-rise construction.

I repeat the ritual, fighting to relax. I close my eyes until I can visualize myself surrounded by white light. Then I gaze into the ball. To my surprise, the mist is there, or at least it really looks that way in this lighting, and so are the shadows, but it's hard to make out any definite shape.

I peer, concentrating, and a moment later I actually have something to report. "I see a shell. A bean?" The shadow turns. "A wheel."

"He's on a ship," Brenda tells me. "He's on the ocean. You know, seashells. And we had black-eyed peas on New Year's for luck. That was the last time I saw him. Could the bean have been a pea?"

People work hard to make the connections. They want to believe.

"It's possible," I say, still using my stage voice. "The mists are difficult to read."

"What does it mean?" she wants to know.

This is the point where I should ask for a dollar. Instead, I peer again at the crystal and dump the phony voice. "Never mind the pea. That's a reflection from your thumb." As she moves her hands to her lap, I spot the wheel and shell again, or at least I think I do. "What the ball reveals isn't always what it seems," I explain, using one of Granny Z.'s trademark lines. "Signs can mean different things."

I have a laminated cheat sheet of common symbols and their meanings, which I of course forgot back at the trailer. Technically, that shouldn't matter. I should trust in my ability to interpret and not take anything too literally. "Like the shell, it could mean the ocean, and with the wheel, um, together they might suggest a faraway destination."

Brenda nods again. "He said he wanted to see the world."

I'm back to my military theory. I try to remember the meanings from the cheat sheet, but it's no use. Maybe I'm just picking up on her fear, but one possible interpretation occurs to me again and again. Hesitating, I add, "Or it could mean death."

Brenda's intake of breath is sharp.

It's all I can do to bite back the apology. My job now is to decide which way the reading will go—positive or negative. I ask the ball instead. "Will Brenda's son be safe?"

The mists flicker, then rise, and I know what to tell

her. "He will," I say. "He'll visit many places, traveling on the seas, but he'll survive the voyage. That's his future."

If Brenda's son is in the navy or whatever, no fortune-teller is going to bring him home safe. At least this way, maybe she'll feel a little better.

Brenda dabs her eyes, looking more doubtful than comforted, and rises to leave.

I try not to feel guilty about letting her go without charging at least a dollar. Granny Z. needs all the money she can get. But Brenda wasn't here just for fun. She wouldn't have been paying to be entertained by a low-rent carnival act.

On her way out, Brenda asks, "You're sure he'll be OK? Not to be rude; it's just that you're a bit young." She pauses. "Then again, so is he."

"Really, Kevin will be fine." I hope that it's true.

I'm surprised by how much she brightens in reply.

"Thank you! Thank you!" Brenda gushes before rushing out.

"Wait!" I call, but she's already gone.

What just happened? I saw a shell and a wheel, which was kind of interesting, and I tried to reassure her. But I could tell that, as much as she wanted to, she didn't fully believe until . . . until I said Kevin's name! A name she *never* told me!

I replay the session over and over in my mind and finally conclude that there's no logical explanation. Somehow, I just knew. What I don't know is how on earth to feel about that. Only one thing's for sure: boy, do I owe Granny Z. an apology. . . .

Psychic or not, I'm starving and, besides, eating is a normal, everyday activity. Maybe a solid meal will make me feel more like myself again.

I stick a note reading BACK IN FIVE on the sign outside and venture out to score dinner from Aiden. He's the nearest vendor who's hot for me and not so old that it's icky.

"I'll have three beef burritos, nachos, fries, and, um, a large Coke."

"Damn, Tiff!" Aiden exclaims. "You want a horse to go with that?"

I give him a half smile. "Why, you got one to spare?" I don't know what's with my appetite. For the past few months, it's like I can't get enough to eat. I don't mind, though. I'm putting on only a little weight, most of it dancerlike muscle.

I take the brown paper bag and my drink back to the tent, leaving the note where it is. Nobody's waiting, anyway.

Half an hour later, I'm polishing off the greasy fries when I smell something a lot more appetizing than burritos. I look up and am startled by the most extraordinarily smokin' young guy. He's standing in the middle of the tent, only steps away, like he belongs here.

There's a gold *T* in the center of his silver buckle.

It fits with his western-style shirt, black jeans, and black cowboy boots. Glancing to his face, I see that his square jaw is covered with sexy stubble. His eyes are a mesmerizing hazel, more gold than green, and he's looking at me like *I'm* dinner.

I drop my fry. Part of me wants to swat the stranger for barging in. Part of me wants to cower, mortified at being caught off guard like this. Mostly, though, I want to lick his sweat dry and rub myself all over him.

The last thought surprises me. Since my growth spurt, I've generated plenty of interest, but until now, I haven't been that jazzed by anyone myself.

"What the hell are you doing here?" I demand.

"I'm here about the future." He takes off his cowboy hat, like out of respect for my being a lady, and runs a hand through his thick, tawny, shoulder-length hair.

Oh, of course. But right then, it occurs to me that he could be dangerous. We're alone in the tent, the flap is closed, and carnivals can attract some scary folks. "I'm on break. Didn't you see the note?"

"Relax, Tiffany," he says. "Your grandma and me, we're sort of related."

I shove my trash into the bag and toss it toward the back of the tent. "Related how?" Granny Z. didn't mention any family in Oklahoma.

"Very distant cousins," he says, with a bright, widening smile. "Kissing cousins, you could say."

I blink. Oh, my God! He's hitting on me.

I blink again. Oh, thank God! He's hitting on me.

I ask, "And you're?"

He digs into his front jeans pocket, pulls out a wadded up fiver, smoothes it out, slaps it onto the table, and takes a seat. "Ready if you are."

I feel like an idiot, but until now I've made no money and the night's burning fast.

I take a few seconds to try to compose myself. It's hard not to feel self-conscious. "Stop staring at me."

He pushes the chair back the full length of his legs, crosses his boots, puts his hands behind his head, and flexes his chest, popping open the top few snaps of his shirt.

"You said something about staring," he teases.

Again, I'm tempted to swat him. "It's all that chest hair of yours. It's disgusting."

He laughs. "You think so?" Pointing to the ball, he adds, "What else do you see?"

He probably *is* a friend of Granny Z.'s. It would be just like her to send someone to check up on me. I'd hate to think what he'd report so far.

My gaze shifts to the ball, and this time it's different. I don't have to imagine a white room. I'm not dealing with mere candlelight reflections. The world around the ball has faded, but not to white—red. Red, if I remember right, means conflict. The images are clearer, too.

"Snake," I whisper, thinking of Eden, of wisdom and deceit. "Bird." Maybe it's freedom. Maybe it's flight. "Cat."

My mind goes to lucky black cats, how I always wanted a kitten. My landlord in Detroit didn't allow pets.

I rub my temples, frustrated. This reading isn't supposed to be about me. It's his fault. He's scrambling my senses. I can't even make up something right now.

I'm about to look away when suddenly I notice his face in the ball. At first, I assume it's a reflection, but no, I see now that he's wearing his hat. I lean closer, and the view expands, shifting from foggy to—I swear to God— HDTV quality.

The hat is gone, and he's running, his teeth gritted. He grunts once in pain. Glancing back, his eyes widen, his pupils dilate. Then claws attack him from behind. I glimpse glistening fangs as the mists cloud my view again.

"Watch out!" I exclaim, looking up. "There's—"

I'm talking to an empty tent.

The magic of the carnival hasn't worn off for me yet. Usually, it's entertaining—intriguing, surprising, spooky fun. Tonight, though, it's hostile—the flashing lights, swirling rides, jabbering carnies, blaring music, meandering crowd.

I can't find Trevor anywhere.

Trevor. That's his name. That's what the *T* on the belt buckle stands for. I just know it, like I knew the name of Brenda's son. I tried asking the ball if Trevor would be OK, but the mists vanished. I keep telling myself that crystallomancy is much more of an art than a science, that the images could symbolize nothing more than a painful hangnail or a tricky mid-term exam, but it's not working. Sweat is streaming down my body. My blood is screaming. My heart has never pounded like this before.

I jog toward the big exhibits, almost trampling Jennie, the bearded lady.

"Easy, girl," she says. "Who set your pants on fire?"

"Have you seen a guy—a gorgeous cowboy guy, tall, and oh, God, Jennie, if you saw him you'd remember. I don't have time to explain, but he's in big trouble."

She shakes her head. "Sorry, honey, but I'll keep a lookout."

Minutes later, I'm stuck in a clog of foot traffic, and somebody pinches my butt. I turn to look, annoyed but hoping it's Trevor. Ready to spit when it's not.

A pack of losers wearing letter jackets chuckles. Five farm-fed football players—one is chewing tobacco; another sucks on a cherry snow cone.

Any other night, and I might enjoy toying with them.

Tonight, they don't matter, at least not until they split to circle me. I could holler, and they'd be tossed off the lot. But I don't have time for that either.

I take a step forward, and three close ranks to block my way. Shoving through, I knock two to the ground. Moving on, I hear one whine about his shoulder, another about his tailbone. It's nothing but noise.

I've spotted my cowboy in front of a toss-game booth. "Trevor!"

If he hears me, he doesn't show it. Instead, Trevor jogs into the open field bordering the lot and breaks into a run. I follow, faster and faster, calling his name, fighting to catch up. We plunge, one after another, into the tall brown grass, farther and farther from the carnival. With each step, he outpaces me. Soon, I can barely see him.

I trip on my long dress, ripping it. I had no idea I was so out of shape. My muscles feel like they're tearing apart, my lungs like I'm drowning. I push up with a choked cry and stagger forward, moving on instinct. Falling again to the clay dirt, I catch myself on my hands and knees. My vision blurs, and I twist on the ground, inhaling the scents of blood and musk and grass. Am I sick? Am I hallucinating?

My mind returns to the monster in the vision.

If Trevor is in danger, maybe so am I.

Just for a minute, I black out. Then my eyes open. I'm soaking wet, sore, and I can't find my footing. My sandals are split wide open, my clothes ripped into pieces!

I smell Trevor nearby, and, again, he captures my full attention.

This time, I'll sneak. Sneak up on him, low, low, low in the tall brown grass. He doesn't see me coming. Can he smell me the way I do him?

His shadow's lumpy. I pounce. Smack his shoulders. He turns. He's got me—Trevor-But-Not-Trevor—and we roll. I feel his teeth graze my shoulder and I kick, tossing him off, forcing ground between us.

My mind snaps back full force at the sight of an immense gold and brown cat—cougar?—showing off his impressive teeth, the white fur of his jaw and chest turned pinkish from the dust. I should be scared, but I'm not. It seems somehow natural to be here with him, natural that he's so majestic, so magnificent, and so very male.

Trevor. For a moment, I'm ashamed to admit I'm still attracted to him. Then I raise a hand, only to realize it's become a huge paw. I'm a Cat, too, but how?

My mom is human. She has to be. She's not interesting enough not to be. Besides, it's been just us my whole life. I'd know if she wasn't. On the other hand, Dad . . .

Trevor gives me space, purring low and circling wide, while the knowledge gels.

It's funny and familiar and, OK, vaguely terrifying. It's also the answer to all the questions I've tried to explain away. My father was a shifter, a werecat. So is Trevor. So am I. The beast I saw in the crystal was me.

That must be why Granny Z. sent Trevor to the tent—to get my primal juices juicing, to spur on my change, to call out my inner Cat.

Or maybe to find out if my Cat could be called out.

"Who knows what you can do?" Granny had said earlier. I suspect even she hadn't known for sure. No wonder she's been keeping such close tabs on me all these years. After tonight, though, I guess it's clear enough which side of the family I take after. Tomorrow, I'm going to sit her down for *the talk,* whether she likes it or not.

Wow. And I'd thought being psychic was an adjustment. This is going to take some serious getting used to. But first, I have Trevor to deal with.

He shakes his head in invitation, and I remember what he told me back in the tent: "I'm here about the future." As in Trevor and Tiffany, I realize. *T & T.*

I can tell from the look in his gold eyes that he's thinking boy Cat plus girl Cat equals, well, more than he's getting on the first date. Our future—if there is one—will take care of itself. But, as for tonight . . .

Tail or no tail, *this* Motor City kitty ain't that easy.

The Bread Box

CECIL CASTELLUCCI

Great-Aunt Eden is not like my Grandma Susan at all. She's so sour. I am now beginning to understand why I had never met her before today.

Her house is dark and musty, and everything in it is made of antique black wood that absorbs the life and the light out of everything. I can't escape the darkness because Great-Aunt Eden wants me to stay inside. She is afraid that I will get lost out there in Amherst, Massachusetts. It's like a black hole in here.

My favorite part of the house so far is the sunporch. It's the only room with light. It looks out onto the wildly overgrown garden, which I'm also not allowed to go into because there is pollen that I might bring back in or dirt or bugs or something nasty, and she wants all of that to stay outside where it belongs. So I can only sit here and stare at the garden. There is every color out there, but inside Great-Aunt Eden's house there are no colors at all.

"Why don't you come and join me out here? It's so pretty," I say. I figure that it's best to try to be friendly to people, especially estranged great-aunts who are recluses.

"I'm so old and sick," she says. "The light hurts my eyes."

Mom and Dad dropped me off here a few hours ago for a short visit while they fly to Jamaica to sort things out. I was supposed to go, too. It was supposed to be a family vacation, but things changed when Dad found out about Mom and her art-dealer friend. That was when they decided that they needed alone time together to decide whether or not they were headed for splitsville.

So they are in Jamaica, capital of pirates and rum, and I'm in Amherst, Massachusetts, capital of weird, reclusive spinsters.

I remind myself that visits are supposed to be fun.

But as of yet, I'm not having too much fun.

"Do you want to guess my weight?" Great-Aunt Eden calls from her chair.

"No," I say.

"Do you want to play euchre?"

"No," I say.

"Do you want to listen to some piano music on the record player?"

"No," I say. "I think I'll go to bed."

I hear her get up out of her chair for the first time since I arrived. She comes into the doorway of the sunporch, and I can see her real good for once. She's got a long face, kind of pale. Her eyes seem a bit glassy, or maybe it's that they are just tearing up because of the sudden change from dark to light. Her dress is white and loose and has a crotched neck. Her hair is short and silver.

"I'll show you your room," she says.

Great-Aunt Eden takes me to the top of the stairs, to a room that is filled by a canopied bed and a large armoire. But the most amazing part of the room is that it looks like a museum of miniature things. There are porcelain figures on top of the moldings over the door and around the room. Every single table and shelf is covered with small trinkets of some kind. On the wall near the door, there is a rack filled with keys. All kinds of keys. Old keys, new keys, ornate keys, plain keys, car keys, big keys, and small keys.

I go over and push at them with my fingers so that they all begin to swing.

"What do all these keys open?" I ask.

"Nothing," Great-Aunt Eden says bitterly.

"Is there somewhere I can unpack?" I ask, noticing that there is no chest of drawers to put my clothes in, only shelves and shelves of miniature objects.

"No, you'll have to make do with your suitcase," she says.

"What about in there?" I ask, pointing at the dark wood armoire against the wall.

"It's locked," she says.

"Well, maybe one of the keys opens it up," I say.

"None of those keys opens the armoire," she says.

"I'd be glad to try them all out if you don't have the time."

"I've tried them all," she says. "I've lost the key."

"Oh, well," I say. "It's a pretty cool room."

"I'm glad you think so," Great-Aunt Eden says. Then she turns and walks out. She doesn't wish me a good night or anything. She just closes the door on me. I guess Dad was right when he said that she wasn't quite social and that I should remember to not take it personally.

I'm glad the room is filled with such interesting things, because I don't want to cry about being all alone in an unfamiliar town with an antisocial person who is a total recluse weirdo.

I'm not tired, so I look at all the objects that are in the room. Tiny crystal things, small spoons, porcelain figures, brooches, rings, buttons, and the keys. I take a few of the keys off the rack and examine them. I'm thinking that they would make a cool necklace if I put some on a piece of leather. Maybe I'll ask if I can have a few to take home with me.

The next morning I follow the smell of frying bacon. Great-Aunt Eden sits at the table in a striped orange housedress with a half a grapefruit and a cup of black coffee in front of her.

"I could have just had a grapefruit, too," I say. "You don't have to go to any trouble for me."

Mom said that Great-Aunt Eden doesn't let you ever forget anything that she's ever done for you, so I don't want her to do anything out of the ordinary for me.

"No, it's fine. A good welcome for my grandniece," she says. And then she tries to smile. It's not quite a smile; it's too toothy, and it doesn't look real. It looks like she might have practiced it in the mirror once too often.

I smile back, genuinely, trying to show her what a real smile looks like, and then I dig into my breakfast, sopping up my sunny-side-up eggs with the sourdough toast.

"Wow!" I say. "This is the most delicious bread I've ever tasted."

"It's homemade," she says. "I bake it myself."

"Really? That's so wicked!" I say.

Great-Aunt Eden pales, as though I've ruffled her. She's quiet for a minute as she watches me eat. Then she reaches out across the table and takes my hands into hers.

"Would *you* like to learn how to bake bread?"

"Yeah," I say, and I actually mean it. "That could be fun."

She smiles. This time I can tell it's for real.

"That would mean a lot to me, Sofia," she says. "I've been wanting to share my secret recipe with someone."

I'm excited that she seems to have perked up. There is even some color in her face now.

"Let's do it!" I say.

I'm relieved that we have a project, because I didn't want to spend the entire day sitting on the sunporch. At least baking bread will take a little bit of time and give us some errands to run so that we can get out of the house. If I can just get through each day with doing something to fill the time up, then the end of the week when my parents return will come quicker.

"I'm ready any time to go to the grocery store and get the ingredients we need," I say.

"No need to leave the house," she says. "Everything we need is in the pantry."

"OK," I say. But I can't help but be disappointed that a project doesn't equal an outing.

"And we have to use the starter," she says.

"What is a starter?" I ask.

"It's a mixture of yeast and other things. It helps the dough to rise and gives the bread its special flavor. My starter began it's life in 1846 on the Oregon Trail with my great-great-great-grandmother," Great-Aunt Eden says. "It's our family legacy."

"That we're pioneers," I say.

"No. The starter," she says.

I am excited that something we will make the bread

with comes from 1846. That is a long time ago, and I think that is kind of the coolest thing about being stuck here in Amherst, besides the Emily Dickinson house, which I probably won't even get to see.

"Why don't you go to the sewing room and pick out a nice thimble from the rack? I think that would be a good introduction. Something small."

"OK," I say, and follow her gesture to the door at the back of the kitchen that leads deep into the west side of the house.

"Pick out a pretty one," she calls after me.

I enter the dark bowels of the house and open every door until I see the sewing room with its bolts of unused old fabric, foot-pedal sewing machine, and antique thimble racks on the wall. The three thimble racks hang side by side next to the sewing machine. They are very old and made of wood with tiny little compartments holding the thimbles. Metal, silver, gold, porcelain, plastic. They are all different. Some are very old, and some look like they were delivered by the postman a few weeks ago.

I wonder what a thimble has to do with baking bread. I bet maybe it's a trick to get ridges into it, like the way you use a cookie cutter to cut out shapes.

I pick a porcelain green-and-white one that I think would make a good shape in the bread. It's also got a good picture on it of a man in tights kissing the hand of a woman in an old-style dress.

"How's this one?" I ask when I get back into the kitchen.

"Oh, yes. That'll do just fine!" Great-Aunt Eden beams at me.

She begins doing the things we need to make the bread: lighting the oven, taking down large glass bowls, getting measuring cups, finding a pan. I try to help.

"You take half of your starter and put it in a large glass bowl." she says.

"OK," I say. "Ready."

"I keep my starter in the bread box," Great-Aunt Eden says. "Why don't you coax it out with the thimble so we can begin."

I think that Great-Aunt Eden mixes up her words sometimes because she's not used to talking to people. I smile at her to show her I understand what she actually means, and then I look around the kitchen and see the bread box. It's old. It's aluminum and looks like it comes from the 1920s or 30s. It's got air vents on the side and a big black handle that you twist one way to close it and another to open it.

"You have a lot of great old stuff in your house," I say. I feel that it's always best to say things that you like out loud to a person, especially to a person that you've never met before.

"It's been passed down," she says. "Like the recipe for bread that I am passing down to you."

I put my hand on the handle and twist.

I think that the starter is just going to be something in a jar that needs to be kept in the dark. I don't expect that it is going to have a face and that it is going to blink at me as its world is suddenly full of light.

I think it meows.

I snap the bread box shut and stumble back toward one of the kitchen chairs.

"Careful, now," Great-Aunt Eden says.

The thimble falls out of my hand and rolls on the floor under the pantry door. My great-aunt retrieves it and hands it back to me.

"You have to give it the gift and press it into its side, and then in return it will give you half of its body so that we can make the bread," Great-Aunt Eden says. She actually pushes my shoulder as if to gently nudge me out of the chair.

The bread box starts to shake, as though that thing is pushing its doughy nose against the bread box door.

"No," I say.

Angry now, she takes the thimble from my clenched hand and walks over to the bread box.

"Sofia, when your parents asked if you could have a visit with me, I knew the time had come. I am so tired, and it is time for me to move on. But I can't because of the starter. Who could possibly understand? Family, that's who. I knew that I could pass the starter on to you."

She opens up the bread box, and the thing starts

hissing at her. It looks like a worm the size of a cat, and it pushes its head out of the box.

"I'm not young anymore," she says. "And someone has to take care of it."

She kind of wrestles it into her arms and presses the thimble into its side. Then she turns and looks over at me and points at me like she's telling the thing that the thimble is from me. I notice that there are other things pressed into the worm thing. Other gifts. They poke out of the dough like reptilian armor.

The thing blinks its eyes again, it's staring at me. I want to pass out, but its eyes have me transfixed. They look kind and wise and old and unhappy. As though the thing feels trapped in this house. And I know that feeling.

Great-Aunt Eden gets a large kitchen knife and puts the starter worm on the counter. It's squirming and screaming. Great-Aunt Eden talks to it, pointing at me and threatening it with the knife. Then suddenly, while it's still staring at me, a part of its tail breaks off.

Great-Aunt Eden smiles big. She puts the knife down and takes the worm and shoves it back into the bread box.

Then she carries the tail over to the large bowl on the counter and plops it in. Finally she adds flour and sugar to a cup of water, opens the bread box again, and closes the concoction in with the worm.

"That's what it lives on: flour, sugar, and water. Never forget to feed the starter," she says as she wipes her floury hands on her dress and goes back over to the bowl and brings it to the table.

"I think it likes the look of you and thanks you for the thimble," Great-Aunt Eden says.

"I don't know," I say. I feel a little tired.

She sticks her hands into the bowl and starts playing with the starter, picking things out of it—lumps that are covered in dough—and placing them on the table next to her.

"Let's see if it gives you anything better than it gives me," she says.

She starts thumbing the dough-encrusted items to get a closer look at them.

"Wash those off," Great-Aunt Eden says as she adds a cup of water and flour to the bowl, mixes it up, puts the dough in the pan, and watches it begin to rise.

I take the items to the sink and wash them off. Some look very old, and some look modern.

There is a small metal car, a paper clip, and a bent nail.

"I thought having you here would make a difference, but it's just junk," Great-Aunt Eden says, pushing the lumpy items toward me. "You're no help at all," she says with bitter disappointment in her voice.

I put the car in my jeans pocket and leave the kitchen and go up the creaky stairs to my room as Great-Aunt Eden shapes the bread into a loaf and puts it into the oven.

I lie down on my bed and roll the car around on my knee until I nod off. I wake up when I smell dinner.

The first course is a bowl of spinach soup and slices of fresh sourdough bread. I eat the soup. I don't help myself to any of the bread.

"Have some bread," Great-Aunt Eden says, pushing the basket toward me. It smells delicious, and I know that it's from the homemade loaf she baked today.

"I'm watching my carbs," I say, playing with my spoon and my soup. I just don't want to eat the bread. That thing was alive.

"A little tiny girl like you, you have to eat so you can grow."

"I can eat the other things," I say.

"But the bread is homemade," she says.

"I don't want to eat the bread," I say.

"You'll come around," she says.

"I doubt it," I say. "I'm not eating it. You can't make me."

I'm thirteen years old and I sound like a toddler. I don't care. That bread was a part of a live thing just a few hours ago. It's like we baked her pet.

"Maybe tomorrow," she says.

"Maybe never," I say. I excuse myself and go upstairs.

I think I'm being clever about avoiding eating the bread, but the next morning, when I am still half asleep, I realize that the toast I'm eating is the sourdough bread. I almost gag, and I want to spit it out, but Great-Aunt

Eden was right: it's the most delicious bread I've ever eaten.

"About the bread . . ." Great-Aunt Eden says.

"*You're* not eating it," I say. It's true: she's not. She just has a half a grapefruit and a cup of black coffee. She didn't have any last night with her soup either.

"I am too sick to eat very much," she says.

"You don't seem sick," I say. *Except for in the head,* I think.

"Well, I am sick," she says, and then she coughs a little, as if to prove her point, and she looks at me with cold, hard eyes. She's a witch. She's got to be.

I can hear rain pounding heavily outside and the sound of thunder in the distance. Even the sunporch won't save this day.

"My arthritis is so bad that my hands barely work," she says. "So I need you to make the bread today."

"No," I say. "That thing is alive. It's a biohazard."

"I know that you can't possibly understand about the starter just yet, but you must try," Great-Aunt Eden says.

"All I know is, that thing is alive. It has a face. And that is unnatural."

"It's no different than eating meat," Great-Aunt Eden says. "Or taking an egg from a chicken you keep in a coop."

Great-Aunt Eden might be right: it might just be a matter of perspective. Like when Mrs. Tessler, my science teacher, brought in a bunch of oranges that she had dyed blue. No one wanted to eat those oranges even though they tasted exactly the same as regular ones. They just looked too strange and unfamiliar.

I try for a minute to stretch my brain and see her point of view, but I can't do it. That thing is too weird.

"I have lived in this house my whole life," she says. "I watched my sisters go out into the world and get jobs and get married and have families, while I stayed home and baked the bread. I took care of the family legacy."

"So what?" I say. I have never been a bad kid, and never wanted to run away from home, but now I understand why someone might want to.

She has a live yeast worm in her bread box.

"Someone needs to know how to take care of it. This is our family legacy. I want you to take care of it after I die. I need to show you how to care for it. How to make the bread."

"No way," I say.

"But it's the only thing that I have to give," Great-Aunt Eden says.

"I don't care," I say.

"But you must care," Great-Aunt Eden says. "I am tired. You have to carry on the tradition. You're the first one who has come along to relieve me of this burden."

"Maybe because it's a stupid burden," I say.

I absentmindedly eat the last piece of toast as she gets up and goes to open up the bread box. She grabs the starter, and it wiggles in her arms. In the morning light of the kitchen, I can see more clearly the pressed lumps of the gifts that it has absorbed. Great-Aunt Eden brings it over to me. I turn my face away, but I can still smell the yeastiness of it.

"It has something I want. I think you can help me," she says. "If you help me with that, then I'll leave you be."

She drops the starter worm on the table in front of me and steps back. The starter worm looks around frantically, slithering on the table as though it wants to escape but can't figure out how. It slides over to me and looks me in the eyes again, and then it begins cooing.

The cooing sounds as though it is saying, "Please."

"You don't have to do anything," Great-Aunt Eden says, "except give it a gift. Then place the tail into this bowl. I won't force you to help me."

I have a plastic bangle on my wrist, so I take it off and I put it in front of the starter worm. The worm rolls over it, pressing the bracelet into it's hide.

Then it turns around and shows me its tail, and half of it breaks off.

"There you go," Great-Aunt Eden says. She snatches the starter worm and shoves it back into the bread box. Then she comes over to the table and immediately starts poking through the tail and pulling out the dough-covered items. I watch the lumps as she washes them off in a bowl of warm water, the stickiness flaking away. They are a small plastic flower, a tortoiseshell hair comb, and a beautiful button.

"Still junk!" she screams, and bangs her fist on the table. Then she goes over to the bread box and shakes it. "Why are you so withholding?"

I finger the button, trying to imagine what kind of dress or sweater it came from.

Great-Aunt Eden comes back to the table.

"I get nails and tacks and you get good things," she says.

"But these things are better, right?" I ask.

"Better but still useless. Not what I am looking for," she says.

"Maybe you should be nicer to it," I say. Although I don't even like the idea of *it* at all.

"I've been nice to it for over thirty-six years!" she says. "And it never gives me what I want."

"What do you want?" I ask.

"Beautiful things! Precious things! Treasures! That's what I was promised when I took on the legacy, but I get nothing of value!"

She starts pounding and shaping the dough and muttering to herself.

I get up from the table and start to leave.

"Take your things," she says.

"They aren't my things," I say.

"Yes, they are. It gave them to you," Great-Aunt Eden says. "It would be an insult to reject them."

I slide the things off the table and go upstairs.

I wish my parents weren't on a Caribbean island in a cellular blackout zone. I wish I at least had a computer here. But who am I kidding? Even if I did, there'd be no wireless. I feel so cut off from the world.

The next day I don't stray downstairs until lunchtime. When I come into the kitchen, she's shaking the starter worm roughly, and instead of pressing today's gift into its side, she's got an acorn that I can see is filled with a paste that she is shoving into its mouth. Then she quickly slams the starter on the counter and takes the kitchen knife and violently slices off the tail.

I scream.

I think I hear the starter worm scream in pain, too.

I put my hand to my heart to try to quiet it. I watch as she pulls out the lumps from the tail and pokes for a second, like she's interested in them, and then throws them to the side. She takes the starter she has and presses it into the pan and lets it rise.

I watch her as she cleans off the lumps.

The cleaned-up gifts are a small spoon, a glass swizzle stick, and a tiny doll.

"Better today. It's trying to please me to please you. But still not what I'm looking for," she says.

"Why are you torturing it?" I ask. "Why did you cut it with the knife?"

"It chooses what gifts it gives," Great-Aunt Eden says. "So if I slice a part off, it can't choose, and I improve my chances that it won't hold back from me. But then the bread doesn't taste as good, so I toast it and use it for bread crumbs."

"What are you looking for?" I almost don't want to know the answer.

"I used to want riches, but now all I want is the key," Great-Aunt Eden says. "The key to the armoire."

"What's in there?"

"Precious things. Things that belong to me."

"Did you ever think that maybe you'd get more out of it if you were nice to it?"

"I have been nice," she says. "Haven't I taken care of it? Haven't I let it live? Haven't I nursed it back when it was going bad? I have been nice to it for years. I'm through being nice to it."

"Aren't you supposed to put a cup of sugar water and flour in the bread box?" I say.

"Mind your business," Great-Aunt Eden says in a cold, hard way, and turns her back on me.

"But you said that's what it eats."

"If you're not going to help relieve my burden, then you can't chime in about how I treat it."

I spend the day on the sunporch, reading. I don't even eat dinner. I only leave to pee and to go to bed.

In the middle of the night, I wake up hot and sweaty. I've been dreaming about the starter worm. I feel it crying. I feel it so hungry. My stomach grumbles because I am hungry, too.

The water glass on the bedside table is empty. Behind it, magnified through the thick green glass, is the metal car from the starter worm. I look around my room at the figures and trinkets everywhere. It strikes me that these are all gifts that have been given to and given back by the starter worm since 1846. What kinds of things does it have in there still? What kind of treasure could be in the armoire? I open my suitcase and take out a pair of bead earrings that I made at Camp Mills last summer, grab my empty water glass, and sneak down the stairs to the kitchen.

The only light on is over the stove, giving the room a sturdy and clinical feel. I fill my glass of water at the sink and eyeball the bread box. I creep closer to it, and I think I can hear a slight whine.

I take a clean glass from the dish rack and mix in a teaspoon of sugar and some flour, and then I go to the bread box and open it. I just want to give it the sugar water and then go back up to my room. That will save it, and maybe make it nice.

I think it's going to wiggle out, like it usually does, but it just lies there in the box. It's not smooth. It looks dry and cracked. Its skin is flaky. It looks at me and then shrinks back into its box. It looks sick.

My heart goes out to it.

I take it out and hold it the way I've seen people hold babies. I'm surprised at how very soft it is. It presents its tail to me, nudging my hand to twist off a piece. I do.

Just a tiny one. I put the worm back into the bread box and watch as it puts its head into the sugar water concoction and begins to drink. I wait until it's filled itself and curled up in the corner before I take the cup away and close the bread box. I don't want Great-Aunt Eden to know that I fed it.

I palm the piece of tail, help myself to some cold chicken, and then grab my water glass and go back up to my room.

I drop the dough in the glass and watch the pieces peel away to reveal a tiny porcelain monkey organ-grinder. It looks like an antique. It makes me smile. It's a funny monkey.

Maybe the starter worm is not so bad a thing.

The next day I watch carefully when Great-Aunt Eden opens the bread box. She roughly takes out the worm and examines it. She forces an acorn down its throat, slices off another piece of the tail, and closes the box, leaving it with no water.

This time I notice that while she removes all the lumps and examines the trinkets, she doesn't wait for the bread to rise. She dumps the dough into the garbage.

"Aren't you making bread today?" I ask.

"No," she says. "It's too hot."

Then she fans herself as though she's swooning. But it's been raining again all morning, and the heat has broken.

"Oh, too bad," I say. "I really want some bread."

Great-Aunt Eden turns her back on me and continues fussing, so I leave the kitchen.

Out on the sunporch, I pay no attention to the book I'm halfway through. Instead I stare at the rain and the occasional burst of lightning. I can't help but think that Great-Aunt Eden hates the starter worm and now she's trying to kill it.

"Your parents called from Jamaica," Great-Aunt Eden says when I go to the kitchen for dinner. "They're coming home early. They'll be here to pick you up tomorrow."

"Did it go all right?" I ask.

"They're home early, if that's what you mean. That doesn't seem good," Great-Aunt Eden says. She sounds bitter. Clenched. She scares me. I'll be glad to get out of here.

I go straight to my room after dinner. I notice that the dough in the water glass next to my bed has doubled in size and is bubbling. It's growing. I grab an armful of artifacts from the shelves in the room and I creep down to the kitchen to check on the starter worm. It's bursting with weird-looking bubbles. It has a foul smell, and it seems to be separating from itself.

I am filled with an overwhelming desire to save it.

I put more sugar water in for it, and it nuzzles me. I pet it. I stroke it.

"Worm," I say, "she wants the key. Do you have the key?"

It coos at me. And blinks. I realize that it probably doesn't know what a key is.

I press a bunch of the trinkets from the upstairs room into it, one at a time, until it seems to get the idea that I want it to give me a bunch of things.

It starts to bubble, and items begin to pop out of it, clinking onto the counter one by one. A small teacup, a twig, an old ring, a silver penny.

"Keep them coming," I say.

Things pop out of it faster and faster until finally the worm is so small that there is almost nothing left of it. And then, there it is—a key that looks as though it will fit the armoire.

"That's it," I say. "Thank you."

But the worm is looking at me with cloudy eyes. It's so small in the bread box, surrounded by all of its gifts.

"Hey, hang in there," I say. I put my hand in the bread box and pet it. It's too small to press the items back into it—about the size of a baby chick—so I take the items and make them into a little nest around the starter worm and place the flour-and-sugar-water concoction in the middle of the nest.

When I get upstairs, I slide the key into the locked armoire. It fits and the door opens easily. Spiders scurry away; a moth flies out; a poof of dust makes me cough.

An old wedding dress hangs in a plastic bag. There are shoes on the floor in a pile.

On the shirt shelf there is a hatbox. I open it up. Inside are a bunch of letters tied up in ribbon. To Great-Aunt Eden. All of them unopened. I open one.

It's a love letter to her from a beau.

This must be what Great-Aunt Eden is looking for. This must be her stuff. This must be her treasure.

The next morning I don't come downstairs until my parents arrive. They look tired and worn out and not tan at all. They probably spent the whole time indoors and arguing. My dad comes in the house to grab my suitcase, and my mom stays out by the car with her sunglasses on.

I go into the kitchen to say good-bye, not to Great-Aunt Eden but to the starter worm.

But Great-Aunt Eden is sitting at the table, surrounded by floury trinkets.

"It's not here," she says. "The key is not here, and now it's dead. What am I going to do?"

"I'm sorry," I say.

"I didn't know that I'd feel so sad about it," she says.

She presses her finger on the dry flakes on the table.

"I should have been more gentle."

I take the key out of my pocket and place it on the table in front of Great-Aunt Eden. Her eyes light up, but I turn and leave the room before she can say anything to me.

"Ready, kiddo?" Dad asks as I exit the house.

"Hang on a sec," I say. "I forgot something upstairs."

I go upstairs and I get the glass containing the starter that has already doubled it's size.

At least now I know how to bake bread.

Living Curiosities

MARGO LANAGAN

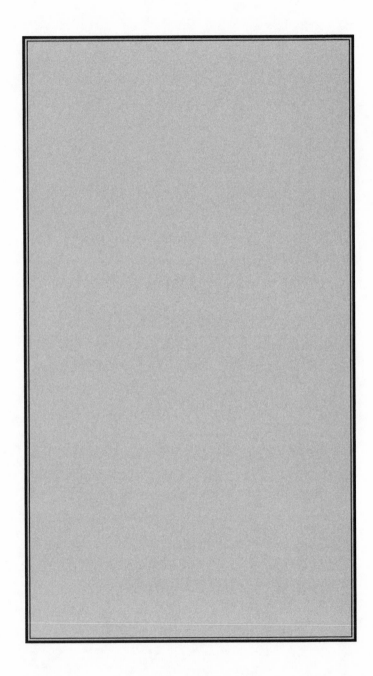

I went to Dulcie Pepper's tent and slapped my hand onto her table, palm up.

"I'm sorry, Nonny-girl. Looking at that, you'll not grow another inch." She reached for her pipe. "Clawed your way through that queue, did you?"

"Have you had *anyone* tonight?"

"One strange young man. How about you Ooga-Boogas?"

"A family or two, and a man—oh, probably the same man as you. Very clean clothes, and uncomfortable in them."

"Uncomfortable in his *skin,* that one. He gave me the shivers, he did."

"Spent a long time in with the pickle jars, then came out and stood well back from us, did not try to speak. Even Billy could not get so much as a 'good evening' out of him, though he did nod when greeted. Mostly just stared, though, from one to another of us and back again. Twice around, he went, as if he did not want to miss a thing."

"Hmm." Dulcie leaned back in her shawl-draped chair, sighed out her first good lungful of pipe smoke, and put her humdrum boots up next to the crystal ball. She is not so much a crystal gazer; the ball is mostly for atmosphere. She does complicated things with her own set of cards that she will not say where they came from, and mainly and bestly she reads hands. Not just palms, but *hands,* for there is as much to be read from fingertips as from the palm's creases, she says. "Where was I, then, last time?"

"You had just told Mr. Ashman as much as you could about them ghosts."

"Oh, yes. Which was not very much, and all confused, as is always the case when you come to a moment of choice and possibilities. It's as bad as not seeing anything sometimes; really, you could gain as much direction consulting a person of only common sense. But perhaps those are rarer than I'm thinking, rarer even than fortune-tellers. Anyway, John Frogget comes by."

"John Frogget? What was he doing there?" I tried to disguise that his name had spilled a little of my tea.

"Well, he must quarter somewhere too, no, for the winter? That was the year his pa died. He said he would not go to Queensland and duke it out with his brothers for the land. He waited closer to spring and then went up for a month or two and rabbited for them. Made a tidy pot, too. All put away in the savings bank nicely—there's not many lads would be so forethoughtful."

I tried to nod like one of those common-sense people. I nearly always knew whereabouts John Frogget was, and if I didn't know where, I imagined. Right now I could hear the *pop-pop* of someone in his shooting gallery, alongside the merry-go-round music. So he would be standing there in the bright-lit room, all legs and folded arms and level gaze, admiring if the man was a good shot, and careful not to show scorn or amusement if he was not. "So what did Frogget do, then, about your ghosts?"

"Well, he tried to shoot them, of course—we asked him. At first he was too frightened. Such a steady boy, you would not credit how he shook. He could not believe it himself. So at first his shots went wide. But then he calmed himself, but blow me if it made any difference. 'Look,' he says, 'I am aimed direct in the back of the man's head or at his heart, but the shot goes straight through the air of him.' He made us watch, and *ping!* and *zing!* and *bdoing!* It all bounced off the walls, and the two of them just kept up their carry-on, the ghost man cursing and the woman a-mewling same as ever. And then, *rowr-rowr-chunka-chunka,* the *thing* come down the alley like always, and poor Frogget—we had not warned him about that part!" Laughter and smoke puffed out of her, and she coughed. "We had to just about scrape him off the bricks with a butter knife, he was pressed so flat! Oh!"

"Poor lad," I said. "You and Mr. Ashman at least were used to it."

"I know. We knew we would come to no harm. Ashman had stood on that exact spot many times and been run down by the ghost horses and the ghost cart, like I told you. It might have whitened his hair a little more, the sensations of it, but he were never crushed, by any means. Stood there in the racket with his hands up and, 'Stand to! Begone, now!' As if he were still right centre of the ring, and master of everything." She watched the memory and laughed to herself.

"So Ashman could not boss the ghosts away, and Frogget could not shoot them. So what did you do then?" I did not mind what she said, so long as she kept on talking, so long as Mrs. Em stayed away, with her "Come Nonny-girl, there is some public waiting." Some days, some nights, I could bear the work, if it could be called work, being exhibited; others I felt as if people's eyes left slug trails wherever they looked, and their remarks bruises, and their whispers to each other little smuts and smudges all over us. The earth-men and the Fwaygians and the Eskimoos were too foreign and dark to notice, and Billy was too much a personality to ever take offence. But I, just a girl, and pale, and so much smaller than them all, all I wanted was to go back to my quarters, lock my door, and wash myself of the public's leavings—and then hurry away under cover of carriage-curtain or train-blind or only night's darkness from anywhere I would be spotted as one of Ashman's Museum pieces.

"There was nothing we *could* do," said Dulcie, "so we just put up with it, most that winter. I went and asked them, you know? I told them how tiresome they were, how he was never going to get his money out of her, that they were dead, didn't they realise? That they were going to die from this cart coming along in a minute. It was like talking to myself, as if I were mad or drunk myself. You just had to wait, you know? The terrible noise—I cannot describe, somehow, how awful it was. There was more to it than noise. It shook you to your bones, and then to something else; it was hard to keep the fear off you. And sometimes four or five times a night, you know? And Ashman and me clutching each other like babes in the wood with a big *owl* flying over, or a *bat,* or a *crow* carking."

"It is hard to imagine Ashman fearful—"

Dulcie sat up, finger raised, eyes sliding. We listened to the boot-steps outside, that paused, that passed. "Him again," she whispered.

"Whom again?"

"Mr. Twitchy." She tapped the side of her head.

"How can you *know*, from just that?"

She put a finger to her lips, and he passed again, back down towards the merry-go-round. That was where I would go, too, were I a free woman, a customer, alone and uncomfortable. There was nothing like that pootle-y music, that coloured cave, those gliding swan-coaches and those rising-and-falling ponies, the gloss of their paint, the haughtiness of their heads, the scenes of all the world: Paris! Edinburgh Castle! The Italian Alps! You could stand there and warm your heart at the sight, the way you warm your hands at a brazier. You could pretend you were anywhere and anyone: tall, slender, of royal birth, with a face like the Lovely Zalumna, pale, mysterious, beautiful at the centre of her big round frizz of Circassian hair.

"Ashman. Fearful." Dulcie brought us both back from our listening. "Yes, I know, he is so commanding in his manner. But he was sickening for something, you see, all that while. I don't know whether the ghosts were the cause or just an aggravation. But it came to midwinter and he were confined to his bed, and we hardly needed to light the fire, his own heat kept the room so warm. The great stomach of him, you know? I swear some nights I saw it glowing without benefit of the lamp! And the delirium! It was all I could do some nights to keep him abed. And one night, I had shooed him back to his bed so many times—I had *wrestled* him back, if you can imagine! Well, up he stands, throws off his nightshirt, which is so wet you could wring it out and fill a teacup easy with the drippings. Up he stands, runs to the window, tears the curtains aside, and there's the moon out there hits him like a spotlight. And he says—oh, Non, I cannot tell you for laughing now, but at the time, I tell you, he raised gooseflesh on me! 'I am Circus,' he says—to the moon, to the lane, to the ghosts, to me? I don't know. To himself! 'I am Circus,' he announces, in his ringmaster voice. 'I am all acts, all persons, all creatures, all curiosities, rolled into one.' And I says—it was cruel, but I had been up all night with him—I says, '*Roll* is right, you great dough-lump of a man. Get back into bed.' And he turns around and says to me, 'Dulcie, I have seen a great truth; it will change everything. I need hire no one. I need pay nothing. I can do it all myself, with no squabbles nor mutinies nor making ends meet!'

"'What is that?' And I push him away from the window, for should anyone come down the lane, hearing his shouts and wondering who needs help down there, who needs taking to the madhouse. They will see him all moonlit there, naked as a baby and with his hair all over the place. He'd be mortified, I'm thinking, if he were in his right sense. Let alone they might *take* him to the madhouse! Anyway, on he goes. He can ride a horse as well as any equestrian, he says, now that he knows how the horse feels, what it thinks. He can *be* the horse. He can multiply himself into *many* horses, he says, as many as we need!"

I love it when Dulcie gets to such a stage in a story, her face all open and lively, her eyes full of the sights she's uttering, as if none of this were here, the tent or the gypsy-tat or the cold night and strange town outside. She goes right away from it all, and she takes me with her, the way she describes everything.

"And he's just about to show me what he can do on the trapeze. 'I will have a suit,' he says, 'all baubles and bugle beads like the Great Fantango and I will *swing* and I will *fly*!'

"And he's going for the window and I'm fighting him and wondering should I scream for help if he gets it open? Will he push *me* out if I'm in his way? And how much do I care for him anyway? Am I willing to have my brains dashed out in an alleyway on the chance it will give him pause and save his life?

"And up goes the window and the wind comes in— *smack!*—straight from the South Pole, I tell you, Nonny, and a little thing like Tasmania was never going to get in its way! It took the breath out of me, and the room was an icebox like *that*." She snaps her dry fingers. "But you would think it was a . . . a zephyr, a tropical breeze, for all it stops Ashman. 'I will fly!' he says, 'I will fly!' And he pushes the sash right up and he's hands either side the window and his foot up on the sill. 'With the greatest of ease!' he shouts."

Here Dulcie stopped and looked crafty. "And now I must fill my pipe," she said calmly.

"Dulcie Pepper, I hate you!" I slid off the stool and ran around and pummelled her while she laughed. "You *always*—you *torture* a girl so!"

"How can it matter?" she said airily, elbowing my fists away. "'Tis all long over now, and you *know* he lives!"

"If I could reach, I would strangle you." I waved my tiny paws at her and snarled, rattling my throat the way I had learned from the Dog Man.

"And then you would never hear the end, would you?" she said smugly. "Unless you ran and asked Ashman himself."

Gloomily I went back to my stool and watched her preparations. Faintly bored, I tried to seem, and protest no more, for the more I minded, the longer she would hold off.

At first she moved with a slowness calculated to irritate me further, but when I kept my lips closed, she tired of the game and gathered and tamped the leaf shreds into the black pipe. Before she even lit it, she went on. "And right at that minute, as if they were sent to save his life, that drunken ghost starts below, 'Where's me dashed money, you flaming dash-dash?' And his woman starts to her crying. 'What do you mean you haven't got it?' he says. 'Cetra, cetra. It was funny: I could *see* the gooseflesh on Ashman. It ran all over and around him like rain running over a puddle, you know, little gusts of it. And back he steps and takes my hands and makes me sit down on the bed. 'Dulcie,' he says, 'I see it so clearly.' And it ought to have made me laugh, it were so daft, but the way he said it, suddenly it seemed so true, you know? Because he believed it so, he almost *made* it true. And also, the ghosts in the lane, they will turn things serious; it was very hard to laugh and be light with those things performing below."

"What did he say, though?"

She struck her pipe alight, delaying herself at this sign of my eagerness. "He says"—and she narrowed her eyes at me through the first thick-curling smoke—'Inside every Thin Man,' he says, 'there is a Fat Lady trying to be seen, and to live as that Fat Lady, and fetch that applause. Inside every Giant there is a Dwarf, inside every Dwarf a Giant. Inside every trapeze artist a lion tamer lives, or a girl equestrian with a bow in her hair, and inside every cowboy is a Wild Man of Borneo, or a Siam Twin missing his other half.' "

Sometimes I was sure Dulcie Pepper had magic, the things she did with her voice, the force of her eyes, her smokes and scents and fabrics, and the crystal ball sitting there like another great eye in the room, or the moon, or a lamp. And the way my scalp crept, some of the things she said. "Inside every Dwarf a Giant"—and there she had drawn me; Mr. Ashman had seen me in his delirium, and here was Dulcie to tell me. All of us freaks and ethnologicals felt the same, and Chan the Chinee Giant was the mirror of me, both sizes yearning towards the middle, towards what seemed long-limbed and languid to me, miniature and delicate to Chan.

"A Fat Lady inside every Thin Man?" I said doubt-fully, but when I thought about it, it was very like what Chan and I wanted, the opposite of what we were.

Dulcie shrugged. "So he said. 'But inside me,' he said, 'because I am a businessman and a white man and a civilized man and a worker with my mind and not my hands, inside me is the lot of them: blackamoor and sav-age, rigger and cook and dancing girl on a horseback. And now that I know the trick,' he says, 'now that I have the key, I can open the door; I can bring them all out! I am a circus in my own self. Do you see how convenient this is?'

"Which of course I *could*. . . ." She laughed, and examined the state of the burning tobacco. "And it would certainly have saved a lot of bother, just the two of us tripping around the place."

"But it wasn't *true*!" I said. "It wasn't *possible*!"

"Exactly. And then I could hear the cart coming, the horses and the rumbling wheels, and I thought, *Good, this will put an end to this nonsense.* And—"

A man shouted outside, and boys. And in a moment feet ran up the hill towards us, and boys' anxious voices passed, excited. Dulcie started up, swept to the tent door, and snatched it aside as the last of Hoppy Mack's sons passed by. "What's up, you lads?" she called out.

"Dunno. Something has happened in Frogget's."

Instantly I was locked still on my seat, a dwarf-girl of ice. Nothing functioned of me but my ears.

"*He's* not shot, is he?" Thank God for Dulcie, who could ask my question for me!

"No, he's all fine," said the boy, farther away now. "'Twas him told us to go for Ashman."

That unlocked me. I hurried out past Dulcie, and she followed me down the slope of grass flattened into the mud by Sunday's crowd and still not recovered two days later.

John Frogget had doused the lamps around his sign and was prowling outside the booth door, all but barking at people who came near. "No!" he said to Ugly Tom. "Give the man some dignity. He is not one of your pickles, to be gawped at for money." Which as there were a number of ethnologicals coming from the Museum tent— as there was *me,* but could he see me yet?—was a mite insensitive of him. But he was upset.

"What has happened, John?" said Dulcie sensibly. I retreated aflutter to her elbow, looking John up and down for blood.

"A man has shot himself with my pistol."

"Shot himself dead?"

"Through the eye," said John, nodding.

"Through the *eye!*" breathed Dulcie, as John turned from us to the others gabbling at him. She grasped my shoulder. "Nonny, do you think? Could it possibly?"

"What?" I said, rather crossly because she hurt me with her big hand, so tight, and her weight. But her face up there was like the beam from the top of a lighthouse, cutting through my irritations.

"No," I said.

Uncomfortable in his skin, that one.

"No." I liked a good ghost story, but I did not want to have looked upon a man living his last hour. "He was *rich*! He had the best-cut coat! And new boots!" I pled up to Dulcie, grasping her skirt like an infant its mother's.

"Here he comes!" said Sammy Mack, and down the hill strode Ashman in his shirtsleeves, but with his hat on. I could not imagine him naked and raving and covered in gooseflesh, as Dulcie had described him.

"What's up, Frogget?" He pushed through the onlookers. He didn't have to push very hard, for people leaped aside to allow in his part of the drama, his authority.

John Frogget ushered him into the shooting gallery. Sammy Mack peered in after, holding the cloth aside. There was the partition with the cowboys painted on it, and a slot of the yellow light beyond, at the bottom of which a booted foot projected into view.

"Oh!" Dulcie crouched to my level and clutched me, and I clutched her around the neck in my fright. "'Tis him, 'tis him!"

I had admired that boot in the Museum tent, to avoid looking further at his face as he took in the sight of us. "Hungry," I said, "that was the way he looked at us. I don't like to think what is going through their minds when they look like that. But he was young, and not bad-looking, and dressed so fine!"

"He was doomed." Dulcie shivered. "I saw it. It was all over his palms, this possibility. It was all through his cards like a stain. When I see an outlay like that, I lie. Sometimes that averts it. I told him he would find love soon, and prosper in his business concerns, find peace in himself, all of that and more. Perhaps I babbled, and he saw the falsity in it. But I was only trying to help—oh!" She covered her mouth with her hand to stop more words from falling out, doing their damage.

"Did you know the man, Dulcie?" Ugly Tom had seen our fright and come to us.

"You would have seen him too, Tom," I said. "He spent an age among your babies and your three-headed lambs."

He looked startled, then disbelieving. "Oh, was he a young gentleman? Thin tie? Well dressed? Little goatee?" He put up his hand to show how tall, and Dulcie and I nodded as if our heads were on the same string. "Well, I never!" He turned towards the shooting gallery, astonished. "You're right," he said to me, as if he had not noticed it himself. "He did spend a time with my exhibits. An inordinate amount of time."

"And with us outside, too, an ordinate amount," I said, holding Dulcie's neck tighter. "Back and forth, back and forth, *staring*. Which is why we are there, of course, so that people *may* stare. Did he say anything to you, Dulcie, that made you think he might—?"

She shook her head. "He gave me no clue. He didn't need to; it was all over his hands. I should have told him, 'You're in terrible danger.' Perhaps if he knew that I had seen it—"

It was then that the girl walked by, towards the tent. It was not someone understandable, like the Lovely Zalumna. It was perfectly ordinary Fay Shipley, daughter of Cap Shipley, the head rigger.

I saw it as I'd seen the boot, when Sammy Mack opened the tent flap and held it open longer than he needed. The world, the fates, whatever dooming powers there were, that Dulcie sometimes saw the workings of before they acted, they conspired to show me, through the shiftings of the people in front of us, through the tent flap Sammy was gawking through, beside the partition, in the narrow slice of gallery, of world-in-itself, its sounds blotted out by the closer whispers and mutterings of bone-in-his-nose Billy and Chan and Mrs. Em and the Wild Man and—

She hurried in, plain Fay Shipley. She stood beside the partition, her hands to her mouth. Then she lifted her head as someone approached her from inside, and—later I hated her for this—her arms loosened and lifted out to receive him, and as Sammy Mack dropped the canvas, I saw John Frogget's forehead come to rest on her shoulder, John Frogget's arms encircle her waist, John Frogget's boot block my view of that other boot.

Then they both were gone. "Did you see that?" I said

dazedly, in the cold, in the dark outside. "Fay and John Frogget?"

"Oh," said Dulcie. "Did you not know they were sweethearts?"

"Just freshly? Just recent?"

"Oh, no. Months, at least. Where have your eyes been?"

She stood, then, away from me, and folded her arms up there. And Mrs. Em came running up to busy-body, so it was all what-a-dreadful-thing and poor-John-Frogget awhile there, with every now and then a pause to allow me to exclaim to myself, *But I am* prettier *than Fay Shipley!*

And, *Look at my hair! When hers is so flat, as if she glued it down!*

And, *Why, I've never seen the girl laugh, to improve her looks that way!*

"What a thing to do on your last night, eh?" said Mrs. Em, with something of a giggle. "Come to the deadest night o' the circus, and look at freaks and specimens."

Oh, I was being so frivolous and vain, with the young gent dead in there, and why, ever? "I don't know," I said. "*Is* it so odd? What would you do, if you had killing your-self in mind?"

"Would you have your fortune told?" said Dulcie wretchedly from on high. "To see whether you had the courage?"

"I think I am too ordinary," I said, surprised, staring at the tent flap.

Mrs. Em laughed. "That's no sin, child!"

"Oh, but I'm used to thinking how different I am from most people, how unusual. Yet this gentleman, and shooting himself in the eye . . . I don't know that I'd ever take my life in my own hands so. I wouldn't feel I had the right, you know? To such grand feelings, or even to make such a mess, you know? Of someone else's floor, that would have to mop it up—"

"Ooh, he's more of a freak than you or I, dear," said Mrs. Em, right by my ear. Her stubby hand patted mine.

I folded mine away from her. I didn't want her cosiness, her comforting me. I *wanted* to be grand and tragic. I wanted people to be awed by me as we were by the dead gentleman, not to say "How sweet!" and "But they are like little *dolls*! Flossie could pick one up, couldn't you, Floss?" I wanted to be tall, to have dignity, to shoot myself in the eye without it taking my whole arm's stretch to reach the trigger. I wanted to be all but invisible, too, until I did so, and to leave people wondering why I might have done it, instead of having them nod and say, "Well, of course, she could expect no kind of normal life," as I lay freakish in my own blood on the floor, with my child's boot sticking out my skirts.

"I'm going to ask Arthur, may I sit aboard his merry-go-round," I said.

"What, when a man has just died?" said Mrs. Em.

"I will not ask him to *spin* it," I said. "It will be safer. I will be out from underfoot, and it will cheer me up, and I will have a better view when they bring the body out."

"What a caution!" said Mrs. Em as I went.

I thrust myself in among skirts and trousers, painted legs and pantaloons, grass dresses and robe-drapes. There is a privacy to being so small, a privacy and a permission. All children know it, and use it, and are forgiven. And "Oops!" and "Oh, I'm sorry, Non," and "I say—oh, it's one of you!" people said as I forged a way through them, pushing aside their thighs and cloths and shadows.

And finally I forced through to the golden light of the merry-go-round. The animals were stiff on their posts and empty-saddled, that ought to glide and spin, and lift and lower their riders; the pootling, piping music was stilled.

"Arthur," I commanded the ticket man nearby, a rag hanging from his pocket smudged with the grease of the roundabout's workings. "Lift me up onto a pony, before someone treads me into the mud!"

Which he did with a will, for people enjoy to be ordered by dwarves as they like to be ordered by children, up to a point. And there in the golden glow I sat high-headed, above the hats and feathers and turbans of the ghoulish crowd turned away from me. I wished the light were as warm as it looked; I wished the music were filling my ears. I dreamed—hard, as if the vehemence of my dreaming would make it happen—that my shiny black horse would surge forward beneath me, and that I would be spun away from this place and this night, lifted and lowered instead past Lake Geneva, past Constantinople, past Windermere and Tokyo Palace and Gay Paree, past Geneva again, and the lake, again and again around the whole picturesque, gilt-framed world, for as long as ever I needed.

JARGO!

Matt Phelan

Now, we had some oddballs. There was Katrina the Witch. She was as phony as a three-dollar bill, but she looked the part. She acted the part, too, even off duty.

At least, that's what I heard.

She never spoke a word to me.

For reasons I never understood, I was given the job of the rear end in the Jargo act.

He didn't say anything.

Not much explanation needed for the act.

The third man in our act was Spitz the Clown.

Like I said, Spitz liked his privacy, so none of us spoke much.

We rehearsed the act.

Chase,

chase,

chase.

Reveal!

Simple. . . .

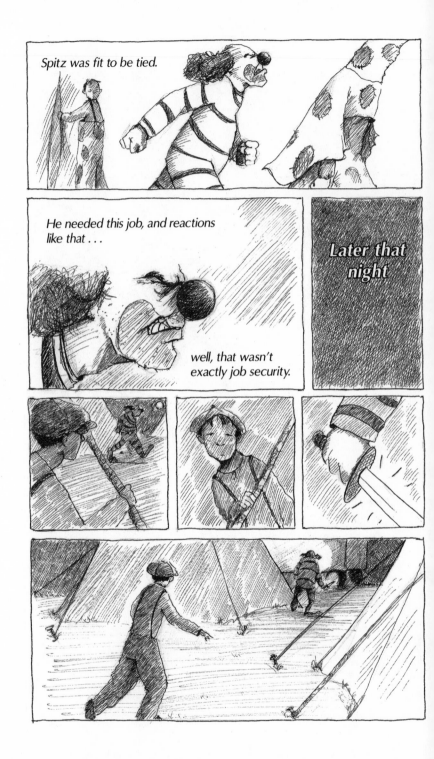

So did Katrina.

The next day, both the Jargo and Katrina were gone. Never heard another word about them.

There are some strange things in this world, boys.

But not half as strange as the **Magnificent Marvels** of the **Manzini Brothers' Circus of Circuses!**

See the Bearded Lady!

See the Strong Man!

See —

★ About the Authors and Artists ★

★ ★ ★ ★ ★ ★

DAVID ALMOND is the author of *Skellig, Clay, My Dad's a Birdman, The Savage,* and many other novels, stories, and plays. His work has been translated into thirty languages, and he has won a string of awards, including the Michael L. Printz Award, the Carnegie Medal, and two Whitbread Children's Book Awards. "When God Came to Kathleen's Garden" is from a lifelong series called Stories from the Middle of the World, set in Felling on Tyne, the town where he grew up. A selection of these stories has been published as *Counting Stars.* He says his sisters wander through many of the stories, "but this is the first time that Kathleen and God have turned up. Dave Hilley and Alan Suddick were real soccer players—and they were nearly as brilliant as the narrator suggests." David Almond lives in northern England.

AIMEE BENDER is the author of two collections of short stories, *The Girl in the Flammable Skirt* and *Willful Creatures,* and a novel, *An Invisible Sign of My Own.* She says she has always liked carnivals, though she finds them a bit scary as well. "In Russia, on a visit, I saw the skeleton of a giant in a museum, which made an impression. I enjoy imagining the world with one thing different or unexpected in it, which gave me a diving board into what it might be like to be a bearded girl." Aimee Bender lives in Los Angeles.

CECIL CASTELLUCCI is the author of *Boy Proof, The Queen of Cool, Beige,* and the graphic novel series The PLAIN Janes. "The Bread Box" comes from a childhood fascination with the starter kept in her mother's refrigerator and the bread box in her grandmother's kitchen. "I read an article about how many families on the Oregon Trail were wiped out when they lost their starter, and it blew my mind that something as small as keeping the yeast alive could mean life or death on the wagon trail." Cecil Castellucci lives in Los Angeles.

SHAWN CHENG is a creator of handmade, limited-edition comic books. He is a member of the Brooklyn-based comics and art collective Partyka. His work has appeared in the *SPX Anthology* and *The Best American Comics,* and at the Fredericks & Freiser Gallery in New York City and the Giant Robot galleries in Los Angeles and San Francisco.

"The Shadow Troupe" grew out of Shawn's fascination with Chinese shadow-puppet theater, particularly its intricate character designs and stylized storytelling. Shawn also felt a kindred appreciation for the performer-artists who were part wandering minstrels and part DIY craftsmen. "Actually, the story was originally about unrequited, misinterpreted love, and the shadow puppets were basically incidental decorative elements. But eventually it became, for the better I think, a 'trickster tricked' story where the inherent supernatural weirdness of shadow puppets takes over."

Shawn Cheng lives in New York City with his wife, daughter, and two cats.

ANNETTE CURTIS KLAUSE says, "For those who haven't guessed, 'The Mummy's Daughter' relates to my most recent novel, *Freaks: Alive, on the Inside!* Yes, it's 'Freaks: The Next Generation!'

"My husband suggested the idea long before I was invited to submit a story for this anthology. I had been complaining that I'd done all this research for the book, and there was still so much good information and so many great characters left over.

" 'You should write a story about the child of Abel and Tauseret,' my husband said. 'You could set it in the nineteen twenties. She could be a hootchy-kootchy dancer.' He even suggested the title, 'The Mummy's Daughter.'

" 'Uh-huh,' I replied absently. 'Sure. OK.' And I added

a note to the ideas folder in my computer, even though I was pretty sure I'd never write that story. *Whatever,* I thought. Writers are notoriously ungrateful for ideas given them by other people, even their beloved spouses.

"I was wrong, as usual. When I heard the name of this anthology, I knew he'd given me the perfect title. All I had to do was write the story. All I had to do . . . wha-ha-ha-ha-ha-ha!

"Anyway, it's done now, and I hope you enjoy it, because I'll have to deal with those self-satisfied looks from my husband for the rest of my life."

Currently that life is lived in Maryland with the afore-mentioned husband and six cats. When she's not writing, Annette Curtis Klause works for a large library system, selecting new books for the children's collection.

MARGO LANAGAN is the award-winning author of three short-story collections — *Black Juice, White Time,* and *Red Spikes* — as well as a novel, *Tender Morsels,* winner of a 2009 Michael L. Printz Honor, and a bunch of other books she says you probably won't find outside of her native Australia.

"Living Curiosities" was inspired by a book called *Professional Savages,* by Roslyn Poignant, about a group of Queensland Aboriginal people who were exhibited all over the world, along with other "zoological and anthropological" specimens, in P. T. Barnum's circus, and by an account of a suicide in a shooting gallery that was published in the *New York Times* in 1858. Margo is 172 centimeters tall and lives a settled inner-suburban life in Sydney, New South Wales, with her partner, Steven, and their two teenage sons.

DANICA NOVGORODOFF is an award-winning comic book artist from Kentucky and author of the graphic novel *Slow Storm*. She is also, on occasion, a writer, graphic designer, horse trainer, soccer player, painter, and world-wanderer. She currently lives in New York City, where she works for a publisher by day and makes album covers, Off-Broadway posters, huge and tiny drawings, and weird flavors of homemade ice cream by night.

She says "Year of the Rat" was inspired by "a New Year's Eve I spent in Jinghong, a small city in the south of China. It was the first time I'd been to China, and though I was traveling with a friend, I felt bewildered to be in such a foreign place and not speak any of the languages. Having just arrived in Jinghong, we wandered into a night market (many of the pictures in 'Year of the Rat' are drawn from my photos of that market), ate fried river moss on the rusty, creaky deck of a boat docked in the Mekong River, and saw midnight come and go with a few half-hearted pops of firecrackers. As we were walking back to

our hotel—a strange green hotel full of mosquitoes—
we passed a tent whose entrance was a glowing, gaping
clown's mouth, and I wondered, What could be within?"

MATT PHELAN is the illustrator of many books, including *The Higher Power of Lucky* by Susan Patron, winner of
the 2007 Newbery Medal. He is also the author-illustrator
of a graphic novel, *The Storm in the Barn.* "Jargo!" was
inspired by an old photograph of a ragged Jargo act and
the memory of James Stewart as a fugitive clown, which
is the only thing Matt can recall from Cecil B. DeMille's
1952 movie, *The Greatest Show on Earth.* His simple goal
for "Jargo!" was to create a freak that freaked out the
other freaks. Matt Phelan lives in Philadelphia.

CYNTHIA LEITICH SMITH thinks that vampires and
werewolves get all the glory. While both appear in her
YA gothic fantasy *Tantalize,* the novel is also populated
with werecats, werearmadillos, wereoppossums, and
were–turkey vultures. In addition, werebears and were-
deer appear in *Eternal,* which is set in the same universe.
"Shape-shifter stories may be found around the world,"
she says. "They're usually about demonized versions of
the dominant predator that competes for food and terri-
tory with humans in the area. I'm more eco-friendly than

that. I decided that my shifters were wholly natural and could be good guys." During the writing of "Cat Calls," Cynthia consulted with her own four kitties, Mercury, Bashi, Blizzard, and Leo, about feline behavior, and they have all given the story "two paws up!" As for other influences, Cynthia says, "When I was growing up, my rather outside-the-box paternal grandparents both occasionally had their fortunes read. I found the whole concept fascinating." Cynthia has lived in Oklahoma in the past, but now makes her home in Austin, Texas, where in addition to the furry ones, she lives with her "very cute husband and sometimes coauthor, Greg Leitich Smith."

VIVIAN VANDE VELDE is the author of thirty books for young people. The majority of them (like the Edgar Award–winning *Never Trust a Dead Man*) are science fiction or fantasy. Despite that, she has never had personal experiences with ghosts, witches, vampires, or aliens (at least not that she knows of). She says she may have had one teacher who was a troll, but that was in college. Although she thinks visiting a psychic might be fun, she has never yet gotten around to doing it. She lives in Rochester, New York.